CVC
9

Carter V. Cooper

Short Fiction Anthology Series

BOOK NINE

Selected by and with a Preface by

Joyce Carol Oates

singular fiction, poetry, nonfiction, translation, drama, and graphic books

Carter V. Cooper Short Fiction Anthology Series, Book Nine.
Issued in print and electronic formats.

ISSN 2371-3968 (Print)

ISSN 2371-3976 (Online)

ISBN 978-1-55096-913-9 (paperback). ISBN 978-1-55096-914-6 (epub).
ISBN 978-1-55096-915-3 (kindle). ISBN 978-1-55096-916-0 (pdf).

Short stories, Canadian (English). Canadian fiction (English) 21st century.
Series: Carter V. Cooper short fiction anthology series.

Book and cover designed by Michael Callaghan
Typeset in Garamond, Trajan, and Mona Lisa fonts at Moons of Jupiter Studios
Published by Exile Editions Ltd ~ www.ExileEditions.com
144483 Southgate Road 14 – GD, Holstein, Ontario, N0G 2A0
Printed and Bound in Canada by Imprimerie Gauvin

We gratefully acknowledge the Canada Council for the Arts, the Government of Canada, the Ontario Arts Council, and Ontario Creates for their support toward our publishing activities.

Conseil des Arts du Canada Canada Council for the Arts

Canadian sales representation: The Canadian Manda Group, 664 Annette Street, Toronto ON M6S 2C8. mandagroup.com 416 516 0911

North American and international distribution, and U.S. sales:
Independent Publishers Group, 814 North Franklin Street,
Chicago IL 60610. ipgbook.com toll free: 1 800 888 4741

In memory of

Carter V. Cooper

The Winners for Year Nine

Best Story by an Emerging Writer

$10,000

Katie Zdybel

Best Story by a Writer at Any Point of Career

(judged as equal in merit – sharing the prize)

$2,500

Linda Rogers

$2,500

Susan Swan

CVC
Book Nine

PREFACE

In 2011, Gloria Vanderbilt founded the Carter V. Cooper Short Fiction Awards. Open to all (and only) Canadian writers, this annual competition offers two prizes: $10,000 for the best short story by an emerging writer, and $5,000 for the best story by a writer at any point of their career.

Year Nine had a wonderful amount of submissions, and in early 2019 the five judges read, discussed, and deliberated over hundreds of stories, deciding on a final ten. As was the tradition every year, the stories were given to Gloria Vanderbilt, and she chose the winners. But in June Gloria died. And then, in the autumn, Exile Editions asked me if I would take on the Vanderbilt role. Out of admiration for all matters Exile, and in remembrance of my dear friend Gloria, I agreed.

I read the ten stories and rendered my decisions at the start of 2020, believing the gala awards presentation would take place in the following autumn season.

Of course, all plans about anything and everything in our lives went awry in and around March because of the pandemic: any celebration of the prizewinners went on hold, as did publication of the collected stories.

But now, at long last, we are all engaged in a slow return to a kind of normalcy. The Vanderbilt prize monies have been put in the hands of the writers, and plans are afoot for a celebratory evening in the upcoming fall, when this volume, Number Nine in the *Carter V. Cooper Short Fiction Anthology Series,* will be celebrated.

"About the storytellers, I have this to say" (that became Gloria's intro line): After deciding that Katie Zdybel (who had two stories in the final ten) was the emerging writer winner for her story, "The Critics," I resolved a difficult choice by deciding that the prize for a work by the writer at any career point should be split between two quite different but equally intriguing stories, "The Oil Man's Tale" by Susan Swan, and "Rapunzel" by Linda Rogers.

A short word about the stories: I especially admire Katie Zdybel's incisive, pared-down prose, her insights into how a girlhood family of friendships can so subtly turn into womanly slights and animosities; Susan Swan has very deftly revealed how buried secrets and deceptions disruptively work themselves loose in a family's history; and Linda Rogers, with a fine rush of prose that has its own music, gives us a witty glimpse into gender war within a family.

On behalf of Gloria Vanderbilt and the publishers, I want to thank the readers who adjudicated the competition: Randall Perry, Matt Shaw, Janet Somerville, Jerry Tutunjian, and Richard Teleky. They have played, in these taxing times, a very special role in the development and support of emerging and established writers.

Joyce Carol Oates

Joyce Carol Oates

Katie Zdybel

HONEY MAIDEN

It is somewhere deep in the thick green and yellow part of Ontario where we stop for honey. The little farm store is tidily stacked with jars in varying shades of amber and blond. There is a window white with noon sun and the honey absorbs the light, slowing it and thickening it into something that can be caught in a glass vessel. It is a moment in sepia – that golden brown, overexposed light that belongs to rural Ontario in August, belongs to honey and wheat and corn.

A woman's voice calls from a back room to tell us she'll be with us soon. Her voice, in my ear, is also thick with light. My husband, David, and I wait, turning the jars over in our hands, gazing into the centre of their goldenness, mesmerized. We finger and stroke the smooth tapered candles, the sweet smell of wax lulling us into an agrarian fantasy.

I can tell that David is imagining us as beekeepers, with netted headdresses and sturdy, canvas suits. We have been roaming the countryside looking for a place – a farm, a town, a curvature of land – to draw us in, let us settle. And while I've jabbered about almost every patch of farmers' fields we've glided past, David has been silent, even sullen, up to this point. This is my Ontario, not his. The part where there is only cornfield, occasionally spliced by towns that consist of nothing more than two dirt roads passing through each other for a brief moment.

A woman comes out from the back room, the fully-expected farm girl in the flesh, complete with cheeks fuzzed and pert as peaches, brown eyes that seem to snap. She wears cut-off jean shorts hemmed with tidy straightness, and a man's faded dress shirt, rolled to the elbows. A pin at the pocket boasts: Verna County Fair: Gold Medal Honey 1991 – last year. Attractive in an unembellished way, she is about my age.

"What can I do for yous now?" she asks in the local vernacular, but without the local twang. In fact, her words seem precise, as though she has worked to clip the curved edges from them.

David looks at her. "Do you own this farm?" His tone has an accusatory edge.

She blinks. "With my partner, yes."

"It's pretty."

She stares straight at him and I know what she means by it – only city people would call a farm pretty. "Would you like to buy some honey?"

David moistens his lips. "Do you just raise bees? I mean, not 'just,' like *only*, but I mean – what I mean is, do you also grow—" He glances at me, somewhat helplessly, and I return a bemused look. "Vegetables?" He looks to me again, growing agitated. "Vegetation," he miscorrects himself. "Or – do you raise livestock?"

The woman looks at me, her mouth a straight line, her eyes sparking in a measured way. "Just bees."

David nods, his forehead pinched. He goes outside.

I lean forward and set a jar of creamed honey on the table beside a tin lunch box with compartments for quarters and loonies.

"My husband is new to farm country," I say, but the words 'farm country' are awkward in my mouth. "We're newly married," I add, trying a different tact. And also, I still get a thrill saying it, though it's been a year now. "I guess you could say in the honeymoon phase, really. Or it feels that way to me."

Her eyes rest on me for a moment. "Six-fifty," she says.

Back in the car, David slides into the passenger seat and fumbles for the road map.

"Where are we?" he asks, more to himself than to me. His tone sounds so reverent I almost laugh.

"Taken with it?"

His finger moves along back roads and streams until he finds the intersection of county roads we are on. For some reason, watching him, I see the map not as topographical but as anatomical. As if he is moving his finger along the curving veins of a human body. Verna. He says the word aloud. That is where we are.

Now he is unscrewing the lid off the jar. He plunges a finger in. A finger that I know from two years of holding his hand is full of tension yet creamy soft, aside from the pad with its bulbous callous from several years of adequate guitar playing.

When the honey reaches his mouth he closes his eyes and grunts. "Oh, God, Sally. It's unearthly."

At that moment, and just as I am about to pull out of the laneway, there is a knucklebone tap at my window. The woman's serious, radiant face appears beside me.

"Did I forget my wallet?" I ask automatically, rolling down the window.

She looks at me as though I'm stupid. "No. It's honey in the comb. It's best that way. We give out samples." She thrusts a baby-food jar at me and then turns neatly.

David swivels in his seat so fast the seatbelt rubs hotly at his neck and his hand flies up to soothe it.

"What?" he says, turning to face me, still massaging his neck.

I hand him the jar and pull onto the road.

That evening we pitch our tent in a campground not far from the Verna honey farm. We do this wordlessly, effortlessly, the metal tubes of the tent poles fastened end to end, the swish of waterproof polyester and the satisfying clicks of plastic hooks attaching to poles, until, like magic, home appears. Afterwards, David perches on the camp chair by our weak fire with his guitar leaning against his legs, while I turn the pages of a book in the domed light of the tent.

"You're not playing," I call out after a moment. I realize that I'm not able to fully relax until I hear him pick determinedly at the strings, as he does each night at this time. There are these little rituals in marriage, I think to myself. And you don't realize how they've come to encapsulate you so soothingly, until they unravel. "Aren't you going to play?"

When he doesn't answer, I inchworm toward the window, encased in my sleeping bag, and peer out. The orange-blue of the fire casts David in black. Behind him the sky is navy blue bled through with black making David's dark form appear as part of the landscape. It is this I love about camping, the reminder of how inconsequential and yet still present humans are, but also the possibility of blending better than we do.

I have fantasies about how things could be. These are futuristic scenes that flash into mind. I think we will return to horses, for example. Well, there won't be cars, that's for sure. Let's say in 50 years, 2042, after Peak Oil, we'll be back to horses. I'd be 73 then; I hope I get to see it.

I think cities will break down – there are no models for cities to run off oil, and eventually, we will run out. But small farms, they don't necessarily require fossil fuels; we know this from the past. They can function adequately on solar and animal power. But we will need to become more humane to achieve this – more attuned to the land and to other living species.

"Do you think we could raise bees?"

David's voice is silvery through the darkness. It sounds different. A lighter tone to it. I unzip the tent and shuffle to him, settle on the grass still cocooned in my sleeping bag.

"Yes, I think we could."

He turns to me, looking startled. "Do you know anything about it, Sal?"

I look up at the sky, place the Plough. There is a trick my mom taught me, about folding your hands into a box, holding the box up to the sky, connecting the stars to the corners, shifting your hand clockwise, and there: the Little Plough, the North Star.

"A little. It's not all romantic. You've got to be careful, David."

He blinks at me, his face softening. "I will."

"Five percent of people are deathly allergic to bee stings. It goes up 25 percent for beekeepers."

"I've never been stung," David says and there's a featherweight smugness to his voice. "At least not that I've noticed. I think they're not attracted to me."

"Well, that's not how it works. They sting out of defence or as a chemical response – the pheromones of a dying bee prompt nearby bees to attack. It's interesting though – a bee usually dies once it stings. Their stingers are barbed and remain in your flesh, pumping out venom long after the thorax has torn away from the head." I lower my hands and tuck them into my sleeping bag. I must have read all this somewhere – these are the kinds of things that stick to my brain, like flies to flypaper.

When I finish explaining I look to see David's eyes on me with an intensity I am now accustomed to.

"Is there anything you don't know?" he asks, and though I can't see his face, I can hear it in his voice, the pride with which he says this, but also something else – it is a hungry, greedy agitation. He slides from his seat and presses his mouth hard against mine, his hands sliding down the tube of my sleeping bag.

Somewhere in the wrestle of it, the clumsy manouevre to pull him into the sleeping bag, the tangle as we try to tug our pants down, there is a brief moment of frustration: it is always this way with David. A burst of irritation – just a passing look on his face – followed by a quick release, as though the tiny catch in him can only be found through a state of annoyance or difficulty. It's so fleeting a moment, and so instantly reversed. Certainly, as we rest against each other afterwards – the meditative pulse of crickets, the pop-crack of fire, the almost-overwhelming awesomeness of the universe spread so thickly over us – I cannot bring it up.

Within a few short weeks David has found us a house to buy in Verna. It's not all that far from the honey farm, actually. We discovered this on a walk a few days after the purchase was completed and we'd hauled our few belongings into the musty rooms of the old house. We had been following a cow path that crested a slope and I saw the farm below.

"We'll have to make friends with the honey maiden," I joked. My hand was held up to my forehead. "It's maybe a 30-minute walk."

David frowned. "I didn't realize it was so close."

I took this to mean he wished we had more space from our nearest neighbour. I reached around, rubbed his back, smiling as if to say, Look at all this land. It was all ours. But then I felt false – of course it's not ours, and I know that. It's just that I also knew thinking that way would please him. I dropped my hand.

On this morning, seeing that he looks at last settled, I bring up the idea of visiting my mother in nearby Clapton. It's the town I grew up in and, for me, proximity to my mother is one of the main draws for moving back to this area and away from Toronto. David was initially opposed to this proximity – understandably. He didn't want anyone interfering in our private future. But he looks at me now over his morning tea and nods ponderously.

"I thought you might ask," he says with a sigh through his nostrils. "I've calculated the gas and mileage. Don't make any stops if you can help it." He arches a brow at me over his teacup. "I suppose there are all sorts of old friends and ex-lovers in these parts for you."

A bark of laughter escapes me. "Hardly."

He frowns and I realize he is serious. Poor David. He can be – well, there's no other way to put it – suspicious. You can hardly blame him; he had a difficult childhood.

I bend to kiss his neck as I clear my dishes from the table. "I was a virgin until you," I remind him, whispering in his ear. He grabs my hand and pulls it to his chest, then tugs it down. It's instant for me: a switch flicked that only David knows about. I slide my fingers under his belt. With a quickness and strength he has me up on the table, my legs dangling on either side of him.

"The dishes!" I say half-heartedly, and so he pushes them roughly, which makes me laugh, deep from my throat. A bowl clatters to the floor, but doesn't break. "Hurry," is what I say next, but as soon as I say that, he slows. He pulls back to grin at me, and I have to grab him with both hands, pull him into me.

The drive to my mother's takes me through slow rises and descents of fecund greenness. The sky above is insistently blue. Before moving here, David and I had been living in Toronto, where we met at university, and married a year later. But it already seems forgotten, our urban existence. I am wondering, as I move through the familiar landscape of rural Ontario, how I survived Toronto so long and why I didn't answer the call to leave sooner. Well, that last part I know – David felt we needed to earn a certain amount of money before leaving our respective jobs. He's eight years older than me and already had a small fortune saved up from consistent, relentless work on construction sites. I added to it once we'd decided I should quit school and started working two jobs. He handles the books for our pooled resources. At the point when we'd earned enough to put money down on some land, he gave his notice and let me know it was time I could do the same.

David had grown up in the suburbs, but spent a lot of time in Toronto. He'd been a teenager when it was discovered that his dad, a trader who commuted and also kept a condo in the city, had a second family. In the second family was a boy David's age. He doesn't like to talk about this, has only told me about it in parentheses. The funny thing is his dad is really kind of a hippie. I met him once – good with numbers and completely despicable for what he did, but also very passionate about living in an alternative way, an urban version of it.

We went for dinner at his dad's city condo, David standing behind a kitchen chair while his dad explained about a loophole for raw milk farmers – selling raw milk is illegal, but anyone can obtain raw milk if they own the cow, so the farmers sell shares in the cows. He'd just bought a share in a Holstein and offered us glasses of pungent milk from a glass bottle. David began shouting at him. He was jabbing at buttons in the elevator when I caught up to him, having grabbed both our coats and thanked his dad for the milk.

"I can't stand there talking to him without thinking he's lying to me," David said. His voice cracked and a tremor took hold of his hands. He held them out, staring at them, then looked up at me. I'd never seen anyone's eyes so racked with raw grief. He stepped forward and collapsed onto me, delicately, his head on my shoulder. The doors closed, but neither of us pressed "Lobby." We stood in the elevator like that for many minutes.

My mother's house, the home I grew up in, is what would now be called a heritage farm home. She would call that nonsense – a house is just a house, she'd say. We had a few chickens and, at one time, a cow, but that was all. My mom had adopted me, raised me on her own. It was just the two of us, the dogs, the chickens, the farmhouse. Card games at the kitchen table, falling asleep beside her on the couch covered by the orange and brown afghan, early morning walks out to the garden to pick flowers when they're pert and hold drops of dew, like diamonds in cupped hands, at their centres.

The road to her house is still dirt, and after following it a while it begins to feel like a pathway, a worn and trampled pass between rows of maples, elms, and willows. The trees bow toward each other in varying angles and postures so that driving past them, they appear like images in a flip book – a stuttering animation of trees that whirl and curtsy and lean. I have a sudden memory of seeing them this way as a child, my head leaning against Mom's arm as she drove us to and from the house in our pickup truck. The gasoline smell of it, her cotton sleeve.

It's been a difficulty for me, going this long without seeing her. I have to admit that. Two years is a long time. David didn't want anyone but us at the wedding, so not even then did I see her, although she was the first person I called on the phone afterwards. I've had to put her out of mind – which I don't like to do.

I like it even less as I get closer to the house and smell the warm earth and cow manure. I feel a sort of dissolving, as though I'd pulled something tightly around me and now it is loosening, just enough that other air can seep in. Familiar air. How is it that smells can do this to us? Rush into our bodies, permeate the skin and re-enter the bloodstream, changing us from the inside out into who we used to be. I play over in my mind all David's reasons for delaying seeing her while we lived in the city: gas and mileage, savings, focus on our life together, no one else's. He was married before, to Bridget, who played guitar and had long hair to her waist, the colour of cherry wood. But Bridget's friends and family interfered too much, David said. They ruined it. Yes, we will make our own choices. Even if others don't understand.

Mom is outside sitting on the back step between pots of orange marigolds, her elbows on her knees, and her chin resting in the cup of one hand. She is drooping forward about to doze off, but then spots my car and raises one long thin arm and flaps it around. "Sally! Sally!" as though I might miss her and drive past.

"I'm so glad you could make it around to see me," she says, after a long, firm embrace. We walk into the kitchen. I smile – that's unemotional country talk; we're both much more than glad. The screen door whaps shut behind us. An achingly familiar smell – cut flowers and coffee – rushes to meet me.

The house looks as though it has sunken into itself since I was last here.

"Are you doing all right?" we ask each other at the same time with the same inflection, and then laugh. She holds her elbows in her hands and leans back as she laughs. I see the gold fillings in her molars. Her hair is cropped extra short and is now so fine I can see her tanned scalp through it.

"This is nice," I say, rubbing my palm across her head.

She reaches up and holds my hand there. "Much cooler."

"David says hello."

Mom nods. "Well. That's good of him. And where is David now?"

I pluck a peach from the basket on the table, hold it to my nose, then smile at her. "We found a place, Mom. Not too far, actually. In Verna."

Mom makes a little gasp and her fingers fly up to her mouth. "Oh! I'm so pleased." She pulls me in for a squeeze and then steps back, still holding me by the arms. Her grip is strong for a woman who looks so thin and aged. "Does this mean I'll be able to see you more?"

"Mom, I can see you whenever you like. Whenever I like."

She looks at me steadily for a moment. Her eyes are pale green, like sea glass. There's a fine layer of water on them always. I think it has come with age.

I notice the water accumulating before she blinks. "Well, I hope that it's true," she says. "I hope we can see each other just as much as we like."

After we eat peaches, drink coffee, and talk, I climb the stairs to my old bedroom. Mom has left it more or less the same. Plain and clean. Full of books. There is an old radio on the desk with its innards exposed – I used to like taking machines apart and creating new ones from their delicate cogs and wires, like knuckles and veins. I dimly recall sitting there, five years ago, playing inventor. The window is open wide and the bed looks freshly made. There is a glass and a carafe of water on the bedside table as well as a tubular vase with a single day lily picked at just the right moment, as only Mom can do, its wing-like petals having just burst from the pod.

"Oh, Mom," I turn to her, suddenly realizing. "I'm not spending the night. I need to get back to David, and the house."

She pauses, having just come up the steps behind me. One long, flat hand is resting on the wall, and I can see she requires this slight brace. "Oh, that's alright. I was just hoping."

Something on the wall catches my eye and I step forward. "You framed it."

"Mmm," Mom says. "It should be commemorated. That golden moment."

The letter behind glass catches the light so that it seems like something polished and stone, as if the embossed words are carved into marble. I feel the same thrill as I first felt six years ago, at age 17, pulling it from the envelope and reading it in my hands at the end of our laneway. *Dear Ms. Sally Maribel Dryden, We are pleased to inform you that you are the recipient of the 1986 Rural Academic Achievement Scholarship.*

This is how I went to York University on a full scholarship with everything paid for – tuition, books, housing, even a meal card. We could never have afforded university otherwise.

The competition had been fierce for the scholarship. Everyone in the rural parts of the province who wanted to go to school volunteered at all the right places, studied exhaustively, and worked hell-bent on their projects. I had created a miniature world – Future Farm, I called it – in which a minute series of solar panels and tiny wind turbines generated actual electricity so that the lights of the small farmhouse – a clean, modern structure – glowed.

All competitors from my own and surrounding counties had gathered at a community centre to set up their projects. A team of adjudicators walked down the rows frowning at our hard work. The house and turbine of Future Farm were set into living soil. I had found a variety of grass that grew in tiny scope, planted several bonsai trees which I kept trimmed, fashioned a simple irrigation system from copper tubing as slender as a flower's stem.

I can still remember the face of one of those adjudicators as she leaned over my tiny farm, her gleaming black bob sliding forward as she brought her face close to the farmhouse window, impassioned scribbling on her clipboard. She paused, her face a hard knot behind her glasses. Later, she handed me back my application form with her comments scrawled along the bottom: "An extraordinary capacity to actualize her vision."

But university felt overwhelming. The city was cacophonous and it stank. I could not seem to find a space quiet enough to sort my own mental workings; my thoughts came out both ruptured and askew. I became unpopular – perhaps I came off as a little oracular. I drifted through the city, feeling as though the streets had been sewn together haphazardly by some madcap inventor; no pacifying, clarifying logic or intelligence at play.

It was during this lonely season that I met David.

A few mornings after visiting Mom, I sleep in and wake to find I'm alone in bed. There's a note beside the kettle: *Gone for supplies.* He's full steam ahead on the beekeeping idea. At night he leaves the lamp on beside me in our new bedroom, his finger running underneath the words of an apiculture guide. During the day he's often out, gathering what he needs – a hive smoker and a hooked tool he calls a "queen excluder scraper." But that's his way. He catches wind of an idea and becomes obsessive about it.

Of course, that's how he had come to the decision to leave the city. He'd taken to my vision of sustainable small farms surpassing the age of cities. The enthusiasm with which I relayed my ideas, while repelling everyone else, seemed to draw him in. He began to say we could build a farm, much like Future Farm, and live off-grid. After a while it was all he talked about.

Yet, now that we are here, now that we have bought the house and a small square of land, he seems preoccupied. Yesterday, I laced up my shoes in the morning and turned to him: "I'm going to walk the perimeter of our property, see if I can visualize where different crops might best thrive. Want to come?"

He was standing at the counter, two jars of honey in front of him. He dipped a spoon into one, licked it clean, then the other, his face folded in concentration. "Can't you do that on your own?" he'd asked.

This morning, I eat toast and then decide to walk to the Verna honey farm. I'd like to buy a pillar candle for the next time I visit my mother, as well as a jar of honeycomb. I walk along the old cow path through purple clover and when I get there, the farm feels quiet, perhaps unawake. There is no one in the farm store, but no matter. I recall the system of honesty boxes in these parts. Farmers leaving their plums and zucchini out in baskets on card tables with a shoebox left to collect coins.

I am standing in the small farm store when I hear a screen door slam, probably up at the house, hurried footsteps in the gravel outside, a shout, and then a cry. I move to the window.

The woman from before is rushing across the farmyard toward me, a look of fury on her face. I look behind her and to the sides of her – I thought the cry I'd heard sounded like a man's – but I see no one else.

She bursts through the door and halts when she sees me. "Oh!" Her fingers go up and comb through her hair hastily. "What are you doing here?" she asks, her voice rough.

"I'm sorry," I say without thinking. "I can come another time. I was just stopping for this candle. And some honey."

She glances out the window and her eyes flick back to mine. "Look—" she starts, her voice angry. She breathes through her nose in an agitated way. "You're – you're—"

"Um." I glance at the door. "I'll just come another time."

She watches me, but still says nothing for a moment. Then: "It's six-fifty. For the jar. The candles are ten."

"Oh. All right." I reach into my back pocket and then feel a swerve in my stomach. "Oh, no. I'm sorry." Now I feel extra ridiculous. Obviously, she's in the middle of some personal crisis and I've made her come down here and she didn't want to and now I can't even pay. "I must have forgotten my wallet. I thought I had—"

"You don't remember me, do you?"

I look up from my hands. The brown eyes glitter.

"I'm sorry," I say, feeling like a fool for apologizing to her three times in the past 30 seconds and having no idea what for.

"You're Sally Dryden," she says. "You won the Rural Achievement scholarship back in '86."

I blink at her.

"I wouldn't be so surprised," she says, her voice serrated at the edges. "You were a local celebrity all that summer. Your name on all the shop windows. I remember your project. It was ridiculous."

She looks at me expectantly, but I swallow back another 'I'm sorry.'

"I almost went through a nervous breakdown pulling my application together. My parents kept telling me to not put so much stock in it. They just wanted me to get married and farm." She looks me up and down as she says this. "I'm a smart person." She steps closer to me. "They wouldn't give me any money for education. Not a dollar. We made a deal. They said, if you win this scholarship, you can go. If you don't, you stay. No more talk of school."

We stand, our eyes at the exact same level. I feel all my breath balled in my throat.

"I was going to be a neurosurgeon," she says, and her fingers rise in the air like smoke. "I like the mechanics of our brains. And I have very calm hands." She looks at her hands for a moment, and I look at her looking at them. "Ironically, this does seem to serve me as a beekeeper."

When her eyes flash toward mine, I turn my gaze quickly to her hands, so perfectly still in the air. She has remarkably long fingers with nails that look as though they've been rounded with mathematical precision; fingers that indeed look like they could cut and sew into the minute tunnels of our brains.

"I'm so sorry," I say and this time I know what for.

"Well. I'm sure you've already graduated, with honours no doubt, and are on to grad school by this point." When I don't respond right away, her eyes pull back to me.

I blink at her, stupidly, and she frowns.

"Aren't you?"

I know that I should just nod, but I can't for some reason, and then I hear myself say: "Well, I didn't – I didn't actually graduate."

She jerks her head.

"I left just before graduating." I moisten my lips. Why am I telling her this? "I hated university," I go on. "All those people there to party and read the same ideas without really turning them over while the world around is changing rapidly. Here we are on the brink of environmental crisis, the solution literally at our feet, and nobody cares. None of them thought far enough. I felt like I didn't belong there. Until I met David." I grin at her, but she does not return the smile and I attach my gaze to the floor. "He made me feel like I was smart again," I say. I'm surprised to hear it come out like I have to prove something to her. "He really supported me. He helped me understand that I was – well, that I was above all that, as he said. The institution of education, I mean. I mean, that's what he called it and that's what he said. It sounds a little arrogant saying it now, actually, but I don't think he means it that way. So I dropped out and got a job and saved up and then we came here." I am still looking at the floor, but I peek upward and then have to look back down again, the expression on her face is so violent.

"You dropped out," she says, her voice tamped.

I lift my head. "Yes, I—"

"Dropped out. And what? Forfeited the money?" Her voice is still quiet, but her eyes flicker at me. "For that asshole?"

"Hey!" I frown. "My husband is not an asshole."

"Your 'husband'," she says, for some reason making air quotes around the word, and now her voice is no longer quite so contained, "has been coming around here the past few weeks sniffing at me like a dog and came here today and – and tried to have sex with me!"

I balk at her and it takes me a moment to find my voice. When I do I can hear myself in a strange way – like I am next to myself, hearing my voice. "What did you say? Did he—" The words cling to my throat. "Did he *seduce* you?"

"God!" Her hands fly up to her face and cover it. "No. He tried to. Badly." I catch a sliver of eye between her fingers. "He didn't know what he was dealing with."

I stare at her, my brain stuck against my skull. "I don't understand this. I'm not – I'm sorry – why didn't you tell me when I first came in?" The words are like melting wax in my mouth.

She drops her hands and makes a sour face. "As in, 'Good morning, that'll be ten dollars, and by the by, your husband's been trying to fuck me?'" She looks at me for a moment and then sighs and says, in a somewhat less angry voice: "He was just leaving when you got here. He went out by the front door when you came in by the back. Maybe you can catch him. If you want."

Her last few words hang strangely in the air. If I want. The word "want" is like an insect flying insistently toward the light of my mind. It keeps fluttering into me. I find myself trying to remember what it is that I want. David doesn't necessarily ask. My Future Farm, really. To scoop the living soil of these farmlands into my palms and press my nose in it. To use my brain to change the course of things.

At that moment we hear yelling. A woman's voice coming from the direction of the farmhouse saying, "Muriel! That guy! He's been stung!"

We look at each other, then run out the door. A tall, black woman with curls is sprinting toward us, a cordless phone held up to her ear. "I just got home to our farm," she yelps into the phone, while waving us frantically around the side of the house toward a supine shape at the base of an elm tree. Beside the tree is a stack of beehives around which a silvery haze of bees undulates, zinging in threatening tones. "A man has been stung repeatedly by our bees! I've just found him. I think he's suffered anaphylactic shock." She gives the address and hangs up the phone and shouts: "We don't have an EpiPen, Muriel!"

Muriel and I meet eyes. She does not look nearly as panicked as the black woman. Muriel, instead, looks sharp, vivid. She is alert to all details, I can see that. It is almost like watching her read the situation. I wait for her to jump forward, apply some kind of immediate medical help, but then I notice that I am waiting, still. She stands perfectly immobilized, focused and primed for action, but taking none. I understand this as diagnostic inaction; I pull my eyes from her and step forward.

I find the pitch of the bees and I begin to hum like them and then I hum more quietly than them. I pretend it is the future and we can blend with our environments. I imagine they might understand me, in some way of their own, at least understand that I am not trying to hurt them, that I just need to get to the human amidst them; and I begin to move through the bees, raising my hands and moving them slowly back and forth as though walking through water. Inside the tunnel of bees, I kneel slowly at David's side. His face is unevenly puffed, like a marshmallow cooked at a campfire. His lips grey-blue. I'm aware of the women saying things to me, shouting, but I can't make defined words of the sounds. For a brief flash I muse that perhaps I am a kind of bee myself. All my actions seem to come in response to the pheromones in the air around me. My hands seem to move without me, tilting David's head back by the forehead, pinching his nose, sealing his mouth with my dry lips. One puff, two puffs. Push-push-push-push-push on the chest. Again and again with the bees around me and their voices blending until it is all one droning sound and the elm tree and David's body and then there is the smell of the smoker, hands on my shoulders, human voices becoming clearer, a paramedic with his sleeves rolled up, arms thick with hair, a needle jammed into David's thigh right through his pants, a gurney that clatters like a grocery cart, the back doors of the ambulance clipping shut, a silence. A silence which fills in a rush with the sound of two women speaking to me at the same time.

"Sit."

"Put your feet up. Like this."

"We should have had an EpiPen, Muriel."

"Don't talk about that now, Julie."

"We can take you to the hospital."

"Drink a little water."

"We'll take you. Come on."

Somehow I fall asleep, maybe slide unconscious is a better way of putting it, on the 40-minute drive to the hospital some distance behind the ambulance. I wake when the truck engine cuts and when I open my eyes, I see through the haze of my half-conscious state, Muriel and the other woman, Julie, with their arms around each other, Muriel's nose tucked into Julie's neck. Muriel notices me and jolts. "I'll walk you to the door," she says.

We walk across the hospital parking lot. I feel confused, as though I had been asleep for days, not just minutes. I know David is through the glass doors, in a room.

"Please don't tell anyone," Muriel says, her voice cutting through the cotton thickness around me.

I look at her for a long moment, allow her face to come into focus. Her brown eyes are like molasses slowly pouring from a pitcher. I clear my throat. "Which part?" I ask, genuinely unsure.

Now she looks perturbed and the eyes flash. "The Julie part. No one really knows."

"Oh." I glance back at the truck. Of course. Small towns.

I cannot find my voice, though I have a sudden urge to tell her that the only thing that should matter in a relationship is that the right things are caught tightly. And nothing else. Catch nothing else tightly. Instead, I nod, to show her I care, to show her I give my available concern to her.

She dips her head at me. It is the first real gesture of softness I've seen from her. "And what will you do now, Sally?"

What will I do?

It's as though some part of me breaks through a skin, standing there in the parking lot: "Leave him." I clear my throat. "I'm going to leave him."

Muriel's eyes turn a deep and sudden shade of black. "Oh, Sally," she says, shaking her head. "Sally, I don't think he's going to make it."

"I know," I say. I feel like everything is moving in slow motion as I raise one hand and in response she raises one of hers, and then I turn and walk toward the glass doors.

The weather turned a few weeks later. The house sold quickly. All the money – a heavy stack of bills – came to me, of course. The money from the house, plus all of David's, which actually was partly mine anyway. I could pay to finish my degree now – and pay for another one if I wanted to.

On the morning I leave the house, the sun comes up a pink-orange lozenge. It makes the hills, the fields, the trees turn caramel. I have the sudden, distinct impression that if I could press down on this landscape with a giant fork, the layers of earth would look like honeycomb and from those hexagons, golden honey would ooze out. It is a sweet, warm land. I pass a field planted with solar panels, their black, glinting faces turned toward the dawn like sunflowers. I turn the car into the lane for Verna honey. It is too early for anyone to be awake and in the store, I know that, but I want that candle for my mother, and some honeycomb too. I don't want to see Muriel again anyway. But there will be an honesty box.

I leave there lighter.

As I drive past the yellow fields I allow myself just one brief moment of fantasizing: Muriel in a bright room, a delicate hooked tool in her precise fingers. She slips the sharp blade into the wires of her patient's gleaming brain. The coiled tubing opens its miniature contents to her, the way a pod releases a cluster of petals.

A.S. Penne

ALL THAT CAN BE DONE

Since the kids left home, Peter and Cynthia Noble rarely eat together. Peter starts drinking early in the day, coming home from lunch at the Legion then continuing behind the closed doors of his den where he chain-smokes and watches TV sports. Cynthia tries to make sure he has a good meal in the evening.

Tonight, she washes dishes while Peter pushes dinner around on the plate. It is almost 9 p.m. and the kitchen is full of the sounds of pots banging against the stainless sink, of swishing cloths and running water when Peter turns to her and asks, "Where did Angela meet this Frank guy?"

"Oh, for heaven's sakes, Peter." She wishes he would eat dinner at a normal hour so she didn't have to clean up so late at night.

He looks up from his plate, brilliant blue eyes opening wide in an effort to see. "What?" He squints to read his wife's lips responding.

"I've told you three times." She sighs impatiently then raises her voice: "They met on the island. When he put in a new door for her."

Peter nods and looks back at his food. Cynthia pauses her washing up and watches him cut his steak, a process he makes as labour-intensive as grave-digging. She'd bought a good cut, a porterhouse, and cooked it the way he liked, medium rare, but nothing much appeals to him now. She watches him lower his face to the lifted fork, close his eyes, and reach his tongue for the offering.

At least tonight he won't tell her he's eaten then leave the plate in the oven. When she goes out some evenings, to a church meeting or a seniors' class, she often finds his dinner next morning, wrinkled and dark, inside the cavern of the cold oven.

"Nice guy," Peter says with his mouth full.

"Yes." Cynthia nods.

He forks a serving of potatoes and beans, lifting the vegetables to his mouth. He chews for a bit, swallows, then lays his fork and knife side by side on the plate and pushes it away. "Delicious, Mom," he says in a flat voice.

"You can't eat any more?"

Peter hears the tightness in her voice and frowns at her expression before giving a quick shake of his head. "I'm tired."

He puts his hands on the chair's arms and slowly, determinedly, heaves himself up.

She watches him negotiate the passage between table and counter, then counter and refrigerator, one hand out for support. At the kitchen doorway he pauses, both hands reaching to the door frame. Cynthia pretends to wipe down the counter as she peers from the edge of her vision.

Peter finds his balance and shuffles through the doorway, heading for the bedroom. Cynthia listens to each step of his slow progress.

When Frank gave Angela a tour of the house he was building, he first showed her the workshop, the only completed area.

The workshop was huge, big enough to be living quarters. And it impressed her that he had all his tools carefully shelved and neatly ordered.

On the walls were framed certificates, and she leaned in to read.

"I used to be a heavy-duty mechanic," he explained.

She turned and asked, "Not anymore?"

"Became kinda routine."

He looked away from her, and she left it alone. Her eyes wandered to an orange tarp humped over something. "What's that?"

He pulled back the edge to show her the hood of a faded red car.

"'63 Valiant," he said. "A Signet."

Angela reached her hand to the roof.

"I'm going to restore it," Frank added. "When I find some time."

She smiled wistfully. "My dad had one of these."

Peter had brought home the special edition Signet the year Angela learned to drive. The red interior had vinyl bench seats with plaid centres, a brushed cloth ceiling and fake wood on the dashboard.

Every day that summer she'd ridden to his office with him, working as a receptionist at his importing company. At 8 o'clock, her father stepped outside to warm the Valiant's engine while she finished her makeup; when he beeped the horn she joined him on the bench seat and Peter backed out the driveway to the quiet residential roads of Vancouver's west side.

Being in the all-red interior with her quiet, sombre father had felt claustrophobic. Angela kept her legs crossed and her arms tightly folded against her breasts, straining to be as unaware of the silent man beside her as she was of the quiet in the car.

"Did you ever drive the car?" Frank asked her.

Angela shrugged. "Can't remember."

"Aw, you'd remember one of these." He patted the hood. "It's got a push-button gearshift on the dash, a slant-six engine."

Angela heard the enthusiasm in his voice and turned to see how it looked on his face. He grinned at her then, the skin on his cheeks and around his eyes folding into well-worn lines that made her think maybe this man really lived life.

Frank had been persistent about staying in touch even after she told him about the other man. Angela considered herself single but only because the other man did not want to commit. He did not see the need to talk about love or where he and Angela might be going, and he did not understand why she wanted to. Still, Angela didn't think it would be a good idea to start something with Frank until she herself understood what was going to happen with the other.

Later, Frank told her that he'd kept calling so she'd remember he existed. And so she wouldn't forget about him.

That first time Angela went to his house, she arrived on an afternoon in late summer and they picked blackberries from the bushes at the edge of his property. Afterwards, they sat on the lawn and talked while the day cooled and the sun fell.

She stayed for dinner at his invitation, and when they went inside to cook spaghetti they had blackberry stains on their fingers. Angela washed vegetables in a stainless sink mounted on a sheet of plywood, then they stood side by side chopping them on a thick slab of maple. Frank lit a propane camping stove and their purple fingertips touched briefly during the transfer of onion, garlic, tomatoes, and peppers. While the sauce simmered, she sat on the other side of the bar-counter, looking at the handcrafted windows and doors.

Frank's house was his oeuvre. It was also a long-term project: even after 10 years of pouring all his skill and much of his bank account into it, the house was a long way from finished.

"I have to keep halting construction to do real jobs. The kind that pay." He raised his eyebrows to check her understanding.

The overhead lighting heightened the angles of Frank's face and shone a glint in his tawny eyes. Through the window behind him a crescent moon the colour of dying embers hung low on the horizon and Angela thought of the other man then: if he hadn't changed his mind about going out that night, Frank and she would not have come together.

Until the summer of the Valiant, Angela had spent very little time with her father. Once, when she had been six or seven, Cynthia had demanded Peter put in some time with the children and so he'd taken Angela and her brother to Stanley Park for a Saturday. Angela remembered it as mostly uncomfortable; a day of trying to read a parent she didn't know very well.

"The war changed your father," she'd overheard Cynthia tell her brother. Her dropped voice and shadowed eyes had signalled this was something to worry about. "Try not to trouble him."

Those words had made her father even less approachable and more unknowable.

On the way to introduce Frank to her parents for the first time, Angela said, "He can be a bit of a jerk."

"Yeah?" asked Frank.

"Just so you know."

At the house, she led Frank down the dark hall and knocked before entering the den. Frank leaned forward with his large hand open and Angela saw her father's eyes lift in surprise before putting his cigarette down and holding out his own hand, older and weaker but just as big as Frank's.

The two hands came together in a tight grip and Angela saw their knuckles blanch, then the quick release afterwards. She waited to see who would step first into the circle and knew it would be Frank.

"Angela tells me you were a bomber pilot in the war."

Peter held his beer can out to Angela by way of asking for another. She left Frank standing while she went to the kitchen. By the time she returned, Frank was sitting on the couch, talking about the engine of the Handley Page Mark III.

Angela handed Peter a beer and Frank another. Frank thanked her but turned away quickly and Angela recognized she was interrupting. She went back to the kitchen for two glasses of wine and carried them into the living room to watch the evening news with her mother. Every few minutes, Angela heard the rise of male voices down the hall.

Later, while Frank and Angela were talking with Cynthia in the living room, they heard a loud crash behind the den door. They found Peter on the floor, confused and crumpled. Frank squeezed past Angela to lift the fallen man, blue veins pulsing at his temple as he strained with the weight.

At bedtime, Frank told her, "When I hauled him up, I had my nose next to his head and I could smell him. An old person's smell. Not very nice."

The comment stung, as though Frank had told Angela *she* smelled.

"Probably all the booze and cigarettes," she said.

She wanted Frank to like her dad, her dad to like Frank. She didn't want to have to choose loyalty to one over the other, but Frank's comment made her think she might have to.

She put her hand on his arm so he would look at her when she said, "Thanks for helping him."

Frank frowned and shook his head. "He's no lightweight."

The day Cynthia calls to say an ambulance has taken Peter to emergency, Frank offers to drive Angela into town.

"No," she says. "He's in ICU. They'll only let family in." She knows she could lie to the hospital staff, tell them Frank is her husband, but for some reason she doesn't want him with her.

Frank shrugs and Angela doesn't ask if he minds.

She catches a late ferry to Vancouver and arrives at the hospital after dark. Her father's room is dimly lit, her mother and brother sitting in the quiet shadows. The only sounds come from the various machines plugged into Peter's body.

Angela leans over her mother to kiss her cheek then squeezes her brother's hand. She moves to stand beside her father's bed and puts her hand on his forearm, avoiding the bulge of the IV tube in his wrist. Beneath her palm, the loose skin over once-strong muscles conjures a memory.

On that long-ago trip to the park, Peter sat on a bench to wait while the kids watched the monkeys. When Angela clambered up beside her dad, she saw the sun on the downy fur of his arm and reached to touch it, sliding her hand up to his biceps.

"You have Popeye muscles, Daddy," she chirped. And when he chuckled, she laid her cheek on his chest, ignoring the prickle of fear that told her not to.

For several seconds she stayed close. Then Peter lifted her suddenly to standing, saying only: "Time to go."

Later, in the bedroom that had been hers as a child, where now her mother has squeezed a double bed for her and Frank in hopes they might come visit more often, Angela slides a palm over the emptiness of the sheet beside her and imagines the feel of Frank's lean body. She remembers the bulk of his bicep and how his large hand takes her fingers, tucks her palm into his armpit and presses his own outsized fingertips over hers. She misses the warm pressure of her belly against his buttocks, her nipples on his shoulder blades and she wonders why such a memory should make her feel sad.

And then she thinks about all the nights she has lain beside him with eyes closed, listening to his breathing pattern, and waiting. Knowing he will begin to mouth-breathe as he drops into sleep, signalling his leaving with a slight puff of exhale.

In the beginning, Angela had let herself sink into Frank's life as though he were a warm lake on a summer's morning, his presence the kiss of water on naked skin. She revelled in those early days of passion and believed that this was it, this was love. Especially after the last, colder man, Angela wanted to savour every moment before things slowed from passion to contentment. After a few months, though, something shifted and Frank seemed ready to release the initial rush.

"You're like a kid needing all my attention," he'd complained. "How can I get any work done when we spend so much time together?"

She carried a fear then, of things dissolving into nothing but memories, the way they had in previous relationships. But mostly she couldn't understand why Frank didn't appreciate the fragility of what they had. She wanted him to cherish the feeling of pure abandon, of giving in to another person as much as she did.

"I'm afraid you'll change your mind," she tried to explain.

"I'm not the other guy."

Angela heard his annoyance and tried again. "It's just that everything's so unpredictable, so unknowable still. And while it's all fireworks and sparks, I want to drown in it, roll around in it. Like a pig in mud."

Frank's jaw twitched.

"What if you get hit by a bus tomorrow?" she asked. "What if I'm diagnosed with breast cancer?"

"What *if?* You can't live that way, Angie." He spat the words out, refusing to look at her.

She felt his aggravation like a thicket of brambles between them, but couldn't let go.

"Maybe I need to know what's coming because of the past. Because I had to do it all alone – cover my absence from work when the kids got sick. Find money for new clothes every fall. Tell them *no* when I wanted to say *yes*. You know?"

She'd hoped, because Frank had a daughter, the explanation would help. But Frank hadn't raised his child: he hadn't held the tiny newborn or witnessed any of those early milestones.

Instead, he'd received a letter from a seven-year-old. And after the initial shock, Frank had struggled with whether to acknowledge or ignore the child. When he finally wrote his daughter, he carried the envelope to the mailbox in turmoil and stood there, still unsure.

"I waited a long time," he told Angela, "before I stuck it in the slot."

Angela pictured his big hands holding a fragile envelope and saw his hesitation at the mailbox. Others would've seen a labourer on a hurried break from work, thick rubber knee pads strapped to long legs in paint-smeared jeans, scuffed boots housing shuffling feet, his visible angst. She imagined his grimace when he let the letter drop and the metal door slammed.

"Did you ever regret it?" she asked.

He bowed his head, ran his long fingers through hair hinting towards grey. "When she bitches about how I wasn't there for her when she was little, how I should've taken her away from her mom, I get kind of pissed. Like I had a say in the matter."

"You didn't want her to live with you?"

"Her mother threatened to send her biker friends after me."

The words conjured a crass woman with large breasts, a throaty voice harshened by too much dope, too much smoking in general. Angela thought about what that kind of girlfriend said about Frank. Then she wondered what being with a man accustomed to tough women said about her.

"First she told me she couldn't get pregnant." Frank shook his head. "Then she sued me for child support."

"You could've filed for custody."

"I didn't know if the kid was really mine," he snorted. "Could've been any one of three guys." He paused, then choked out a laugh and added, "Except she looks just like me!"

He stood to pull out his wallet, held out a photo with edges shaped by the curve of his back pocket.

The bride in the picture had familiar hazel eyes. "At her wedding?" Angela asked.

"Yeah." Frank grinned and Angela saw him flush. With pride?

His goofy response drew an equally strange one from her, a light-headedness as though she might swoon. And when she looked back at the photo, she found herself envious of the young girl in the picture.

Frank ranted some more about his daughter's mother, then started about two other former girlfriends.

"Both big mistakes," he concluded.

"But you must have learned something?" Angela asked.

"Yeah – you have to be able to communicate with your partner."

She stared, trying to decide whether he was oblivious to the irony of the statement or had simply gone somewhere else in his thoughts.

"Ellen would just walk away in the middle of a discussion, and Laura screamed or threw things," he snorted.

Angela had never seen pictures of Frank's previous lovers. Without names, they'd seemed anonymous and unofficial. Now Ellen and Laura took on substance: Frank mentioned Ellen's German roots and Angela pictured a buxom blonde. Laura, as tall as Frank, rode horses, conjuring a muscular and slightly broad-in-the-beam body. And then she caught herself.

"You know what?" she interrupted. "I don't need to know who they are. That's kind of private, like what happened between you and them."

Frank looked surprised.

"Just in case I ever meet them," Angela explained. "I don't want to be thinking, 'Oh, *you're* the one that screams and throws things.' You know?"

Frank shook his head. "Trust me. You're never going to meet them."

Afterwards, she wondered if he'd repeated things to Ellen and Laura, the way he did to her.

"We're good together," he'd said over and over. "We're good in bed, we can talk, we both like lots of alone time. It's a good match."

Was he trying to persuade himself?

In the hospital room with clicking ventilation machinery, Angela watches the Herculean fight of her father's respiratory system. With each in-breath, the old man's diaphragm heaves an invisible weight and a monitor graphs the crumpling of his brow, 19 times per minute. Only at the *whoosh* of exhalation does his forehead smooth.

Cynthia's voice is small and weak when she speaks now. "I've told the doctor not to… to resuscitate him if…" She stops, then finishes in a rush: "…there's an emergency situation."

Angela avoids looking at her mother – she does not want to witness the begging in her eyes – and only nods with slow acceptance. Nobody wants to take Peter home in this helpless state, a man who can't talk at the best of times and who may never again be able to talk anyway.

When her mother and brother go for coffee, Angela sits in a corner of the room, wondering at the distance between herself and her father as his frown pinches then lets go. Twice she rises from her chair to go to his bedside and put her cool palm on the back of his hand. At those times she wants to lean over the bed rail and whisper in his ear, tell him everything is all right, not to be afraid. But she isn't sure he can hear her; or that he is listening.

The quiet morning drives with Peter had been an exercise in endurance. Angela had focused on the markers of the daily route to avoid hearing the deafening silence in the car.

There was the stunning view of the heat-hazed city, a postcard vista of ocean, and mountains, and skyscrapers as the car slid down the hill of 4th Avenue. The black and red freighters glimpsed between the tall privacy hedges of Point Grey Road homes. Kitsilano Beach with its wide stretch of sand separating Burrard Inlet from dog walkers and joggers. And when the Valiant rolled to a stop behind traffic waiting at the intersection before the bridge, they sat in the sear of morning sun and felt the oven-like sizzle of the red vinyl interior. Peter pushed in the cigarette lighter and rolled down the window. When the light turned green, they joined the leap of cars crowding onto the bridge.

At the top of the span, a blaze of light lanced the windshield and Angela stared out the passenger window. Shifting to peel her bare legs off the vinyl seat, she found the last marker, the billboard that was the gatekeeper to the downtown.

At the end of a long, tiring week for both of them, Angela and Frank sit quietly on the deck to watch the sunset.

Angela sighs loudly.

"What?" Franks asks.

"I know it can't always be electric," she begins, "but doesn't it feel like we're already this old married couple with nothing to say to each other?"

Frank's head turns slowly and his eyes, when they lock on hers, aren't the warm hazel she loves.

"Has anyone ever told you you're too analytical?"

A hot flush crosses her cheeks and Angela looks down. "I don't want to end up like my mom and dad, is all."

"Keep it light. I know you want to talk, but sometimes I'm too fucking tired at the end of a workday to get into a big thing and then you're all upset because you think I'm being uncommunicative."

Sometimes at night when she's lying beside Frank and listening to his breathing, Angela replays their conversations in her head. When she thinks about uncomfortable words they've exchanged, she has an image of Frank giving her a look of disgust; of herself begging.

"You're taking the fun out of this for me," Frank says when she tries, again, to talk about things.

What about the fun in it for me? she wants to ask, but does not. She doesn't want to start what Frank would call – the day after, when he's calmer and sorry about another fight – a "discussion." To Angela those "discussions" are destructive, becoming situations where Frank turns into a steam train, bulldozing everything off the tracks, including her.

What bothers her most is that she feels like a fake. When she can't tell him how she feels – when he can't listen – she has to pretend she's someone else altogether. Someone easy-going and happy.

Angela would like to be able to manage the ongoing disquiet in her life. She needs to take better control of her emotions: she is crying too often these days, because of her father's illness but also because of the turbulence with Frank.

She reads about Zen meditation techniques and learns that her feelings of urgency are not real, not worthy of holding. She has never been able to meditate before, but now when she observes her feelings, notes them then lets them go, she feels as though she could learn to be as calm and detached as any Tibetan monk.

She becomes less affected by whether Frank is able to hear her concerns; by whether they spend time together or apart. He is somewhere out there, and that is reassuring in a small way, though his company begins to seem like the silence of her father's in the old Valiant – beside her, but not with her.

"What's wrong?" Frank asks one night.

"Nothing."

"Come on. Something's bugging you."

"I'm fine. Really."

"Why don't you want to talk about it?"

"Because we'll get in an argument over it."

"Aw, Angie – not again."

Angela shrugs.

"Look, in any relationship you take the good with the bad," Frank says. "It's like your mom and dad."

Angela swings around to face him. "And the good they have is....?"

He shakes his head at her, incredulous, holds his hands open. "It's the company. Your mom isn't alone and neither is your dad."

Angela's eyebrows go up. "They live separate lives under the same roof. Is that 'company'?"

"You always look at the negative side of things."

Angela thought her assessment was pretty realistic. Was it too much to want a partner to pay attention the way they had when they started? In those first months, Frank had stayed awake all night with her. Now he falls asleep after dinner on the nights they spend together.

He's annoyed when she brings it up. "What do you expect? I work a physical job. I'm tired at the end of the day. I need downtime."

It was another "discussion" leading to a repetitive argument. Frank accused Angela of needing him to fill her free time, but that complaint didn't hold water for her: he knew she cherished her alone time, so why did he feel cornered?

Angela wonders if it scares Frank, seeing how much Peter needs from Cynthia; if he thinks one day he might need that kind of care himself. Or that he may have to provide it for her.

The cardiac surgeon was younger than Angela. He spoke carefully, but with authority in a heavy Australian accent, choosing words that would not compromise either himself or the hospital.

"Don't get me wrong," he said. "He's a very sick man. But he's stabilized somewhat and I'm hoping he'll be able to go home next week."

The family stood in a half-circle round the bed, watching the creasing of Peter's brow each time his lungs strained. It was an effort to believe that body would be able to get up, move and function again.

Later, Angela sat alone by the window and stared at the distant panorama of mountains and sea. When the door opened and a young woman entered with a walker, Angela raised her eyebrows with a question.

"I'm from Physio," the woman smiled.

Angela shook her head, surprised. "You want to get him up?"

"He needs to use his muscles."

"He can hardly breathe and he can't even feed himself," Angela protested. "How is he going to stand?"

"They'll atrophy otherwise. Cause more problems." She went to the bedside and called to Peter as though he were on a mountain top, far away: "Mr. Noble? Wake up, Mr. Noble. It's time for your exercise."

"He's drugged to the hilt..."

The therapist pressed a lever to bring the bed upright, and Peter's eyelids opened above the oxygen mask. He stared uncomprehendingly, and when his blue irises found Angela, she saw his stark fear. She swallowed the stone in her throat and forced a smile.

Angela flinched at the too-loud and too-precise voice of the physio, turning away from the slow and patronizing manipulation of Peter from the bed to a chair. When she glanced back, she saw his hands clinging white-knuckled to the walker and a hot rise of tears unseated her.

"Let's move those feet, Mr. Noble," shouted the therapist.

Peter's right foot shot forward. He stood, wobbling, then the left foot jerked forward.

For a second it seemed he was done, ready to collapse, and then he repeated the motion. Right foot, wobble; left foot, pause. And a third time.

Angela held her breath, watching the stuttering traverse of the room, stunned at Peter's bullish determination.

At the door, he stopped and reached for the handle.

"That's far enough, Mr. Noble," chortled the physio. "My! Your daughter thought you weren't strong enough to get out of bed, but I guess you proved her wrong, didn't you?"

After another half hour of adjusting tubes and monitor feeds, Peter's head sank back on the pillow, and he slipped into sleep.

When the physio was gone, Angela moved to the bedside and laid a hand on his covered shin. Beneath her palm she felt the warmth of blood and life.

"Bye, Pop," she whispered.

The old eyes blinked open, unfocused. Angela smiled back hopefully. Peter's right hand lifted slowly, as if to wave goodbye. His mouth opened.

Angela waited.

His eyes closed.

The lids flickered. Angela's breathing slowed.

Peter's eyes opened and found hers. He opened his mouth and his voice came, hoarse but clear.

"Thanks." The blue eyes held hers for two long seconds. Then his hand dropped and the eyelids shut.

She waited, blinking through tears, holding her breath.

Frank is already asleep when Angela arrives home from the ferry. The longer days mean he gets up at dawn so he can work extra hours on building sites.

But it is only dusk and after the emotional drain of the hospital and the hours of travel, Angela is too wound up to go to bed. Lately, she has been plagued by insomnia, and besides, going to bed when it is still light outside seems unnatural.

The only time she and Frank spend together now is at dinner on those days when Angela isn't in the city.

One night she buys fresh seafood and good wine and sets the table outside in the coolness of the back garden. She waits until she hears his truck in the driveway and then she pours him a glass of wine and carries it out to greet him. She takes him by the hand and leads him to the garden table.

"Looks great, babe," he says, nuzzling her cheek with day-old stubble. He groans in tiredness as he sits down.

Angela stands behind him, massaging his neck and shoulders as he relaxes into the wine and the pleasure of her attention. After a minute she steps around his chair and sits sideways on his lap, stretching her arms around his neck and pressing her nose against his. "Wanna have some fun tonight, pardner?"

He grins at her, massaging her behind with his big hand. "*May*be." He kisses her earlobe. "Depends how good dinner is," he jibes.

She stands as if to go then lifts her leg to straddle him. She puts her fingers on his shirt buttons and looks him in the eye as she starts to undo them. "Hey – food first," he says, grabbing her wrists.

"How do you know there is any?"

"C'mon, hon. I'm all stinky from work."

"I like you stinky." She frees her hands and goes for his fly.

"No, ma'am. You have to feed your man before you get any of that!"

He puts his hands on her waist and lifts her to a standing position.

Angela hesitates, then sits down beside him. And when she feels the rough working hand reaching for her smoother one, she turns to him. He is smiling at her with eyes that send a message she can't translate. She knows she is supposed to accept this gift with some kind of grace, but she cannot. She does not know how to banish the surge of pure want – of need – rising inside. It's a need of comfort or of sustenance; something she can't have or he can't give.

The urgency is unrestrained and wild. She knows this feeling, remembers it from those summer car rides with her father.

Peter's slow driving combined with the silence in the car unbalanced her. It was all she could do not to lean over and honk the horn, wave at other drivers to let them know it wasn't her driving so tediously. So when the Valiant dropped down the other side of the bridge and the familiar billboard with its orange and black tug came into view, she was already tense.

The old tug had sailed the curled blue crests of motorized waves for as long as she could remember, bookending rare family excursions into downtown for shopping or movies. Inside the wheelhouse of the lifting and rolling tug was an always-smiling captain, a Santa Claus look-alike with rosy complexion and chubby cheeks whose cheerfulness was so different from her father's unfathomable expression.

Then one morning the Valiant crested the bridge and her father leaned forward to squint at the billboard.

"I always wondered," Peter began, then stopped to clear the rust from his throat, "if that little man gets seasick."

Angela had stared first at her father then at the billboard to make sure she understood the reference. When she looked again at Peter, his silent profile the same as always, unmoved and unapproachable, she laughed.

But the laugh came out wrong, a harsh barking sound, and much too loud. It was not the response she meant, but it was all she had.

Angela and her mother are already in bed when the phone rings. She hears Cynthia answer and then the surprise in her mother's voice.

"But he was fine when we left a little while ago…"

Angela does not wait to be told. She is up and dressed by the time her mother is off the phone.

"I'll start the car," she says, searching her mother's eyes. She sees no fear there; no apparent loss of calm.

Warming the car, Angela remembers her last visit to Frank's.

She'd opened the door of the workshop and called when she didn't see him. "Frank?"

The toilet flushed and he came out zipping his fly. "Hey!" he smiled, then nodded at something over her shoulder. "Look."

Angela turned and saw the uncovered Valiant with its hood propped open.

She walked over to peer at the engine cavity as Frank wrapped his arms around her from behind.

"Whaddaya think?" he asked.

The amount of space under the hood was a surprise. But simplicity was Frank's preference, that much she knew. She spun in his arms to kiss him, then asked, "Thought you were going to wait 10 years to do it?"

"I know but… "

He dropped his hands and wiped them on his jeans. "I was thinking about your dad and how he's… His war years and stuff." He stepped forward, leaned crossed arms on the fender and stared at the engine. "I thought you might like it as a momento."

Angela smiled. "Memento."

"Huh?"

She put a hand on his shoulder. "But this was going to be your baby."

Frank shrugged. "It's only if I can get it going, though." He nodded, patted the fender then stood to open the driver's door. "Get in. See how it feels."

When she folded herself onto the vinyl bench seat, there it was again – the redness of the interior on that long-ago summer's day.

"Yeah?" Frank asked as she gripped the skinny plastic steering wheel.

"Yeah," she breathed.

The moon is almost full, the skies as pure as ink and at every intersection Angela hits a red light. Beside her, Cynthia seems quiet, alert but unflustered.

At the hospital, they are delayed by security officers wanting identification for after-hours entrance, and it is not until they stand waiting for the elevator to take them to the cardiac unit that Angela accepts what is happening, why they are back here.

They walk the ward corridor, see the nursing station in the distance and Angela identifies the nurse watching their approach. She knows, and she thinks that her mother must know, what the nurse's look means.

The doctor comes out of her father's room before they can reach the open doorway. He is soft-spoken and calm when he says, "I'm sorry."

Angela puts her hand on her mother's shoulder but there is no tremble, no sign of distress.

"Do you want to see him?" the doctor asks.

Inside the room, there is nothing to suggest a struggle with death; no rumpled sheets or emergency medical machinery. Just her father's body lying with eyes shut and mouth slightly open. Angela stands on one side of the bed and her mother stands on the other, and Cynthia puts her palm on her husband's forehead.

"He's still warm," she says, raising tired, grey eyes to Angela's.

After a few dazed minutes, Cynthia leaves the room to phone the minister and Angela looks carefully at her father's closed face. She isn't sure what she should do or how to say goodbye and so she whispers into the quiet of the room.

"Thanks for the good stuff," she tells the body. He looks the same as always, grumpy and tired and silent.

At the funeral, Frank sits with her brother and other pallbearers, and Angela sits across the aisle with Cynthia. The flag-draped coffin stands before them, so close that Angela could touch the plain pine box. Without trying too hard, she can picture her father lying on his back, his Legionnaire beret above closed eyes, lined face serene at last. She imagines how it must feel inside the coffin, its inky blackness so final and complete.

The organ's first chords and the whispering sound of the congregation coming to their feet cue her automatic response. As she stands, Angela looks for Frank, finds his dark head towering above her brother and nephews; and as if he's heard her, as if she's called him, Frank tilts his head and smiles quizzically.

In that moment his presence is enough, the distance between them less incomprehensible.

For a second, she understands that in this life there is only the opportunity to open fully to someone and hope they may also open in return.

She turns back to the front and lifts her arm around the old lady beside her, clutching like a small child.

Christine Ottoni

PLASTIC

After I made the decision to get the operation, I asked Moira to meet me for a drink.

"You can't be serious," she said, after I'd told her.

"I am."

"Why?"

"You know why," I muttered and sipped the cocktail Moira had ordered for me. Something sweet with gin and egg white. At first, I'd asked the bartender for a cranberry soda, but Moira cut across me. She hated drinking alone. I liked knowing little things like that about Moira, all the eccentricities that made her a whole person. Her favourite dinner was crackers and cheese. She lost her virginity in a tent during a thunderstorm. I never expected to have a best friend, but Moira and I just ended up that way. Like two orphans fighting over a bone in the street only to look up and find we had more in common than we'd originally thought.

"Which parts?" Moira gave me the up and down, considering my nose, fingers, shoulders, and stomach. What I'd be willing to part with. "Not more than one?"

"No," I said. "Just a specific area."

We both knew what area I meant. That made Moira quiet. She considered me for a minute, chewing her lip, deciding if she should start arguing with me now or later.

"What material are you choosing?"

"Plastic."

"Why?"

I shrugged. "It feels right."

Moira loved me fiercely, but she never understood my issue with the area in question. She couldn't. Moira wasn't religious – she was raised agnostic – but she was, in a way, a bit of a zealot when it came to sex. She believed in the beauty of it, its cosmic humanity. Every fuck, for her, was an acid trip to the moon. And that made the central drama of my adult life totally unfathomable to her.

Moira had stick and poke tattoos scattered up her legs and arms, in places where she could reach to do them herself with a needle and ink. Among the collection on her forearms: a watermelon slice, a rocking chair, a viper. She grabbed my hand across the table.

"You can't do it," she said.

"Come on."

"You're giving up."

I pulled my hand back.

I couldn't meet her eyes. Moira always believed I could work past my problem. More therapy, more medication, the right exposure. *Just put yourself out there, practice makes perfect*, that kind of thing. But when operations and replacements started becoming more common, when it wasn't just ads in the subway anymore, but people walking around with synthetic gold toes or hot pink silicone kneecaps, I couldn't get the idea out of my head. I wanted the operation. I wanted my problem, the area, to become plastic. Smooth and forgiving. Unfeeling. Like a doll or silvery android from a movie. Something unformed in alien utero without a name or a purpose.

We sat like that for a while. I stared down at my drink until Moira sighed, breaking the silence.

"Fine," she said. She leaned forward and picked up her drink. "To your flesh."

Moira didn't give up so easily, that wasn't her style, and in the morning she called to announce, in a decidedly offhand manner, that she was going to throw a party. "It's been a while, you know?"

That was the kind of thing Moira did in a crisis. She didn't say the party would be my last hurrah, my last chance to get laid, to change my mind, but really that's what she meant by it. I'd been through this with Moira before. *This is John, from the camera department. Nick, he's a gaffer.* By then I was practiced at polite disinterest, at turning them down in clear terms. I'd never be able to give them what they wanted – a girl who would push them against the wall and slip her tongue in their ear. A girl who jumped into bed, all night having perfect pink orgasms.

Moira wanted an opportunity to save me from myself, if she could, and I gave in and told her I'd go to the party, at least for a couple hours. It wouldn't change anything. I was already booked in for my pre-op, I'd done all my bloodwork and tests, passed my psych evaluation with flying colours.

"Of course, this will be the first of this kind of replacement on Canadian soil," the doctor had said.

We had been sitting in her office sipping green tea from small clay bowls. Her assistant had brought them in. The doctor was behind her desk, blowing on her tea to cool it down. I held my bowl under my chin, lips pursed, blowing, mirroring her serene exterior.

"Oh yes, I heard that," I said.

"I assisted with one in the Netherlands," she went on. "It was a young girl, a case very similar to yours. Trauma. Before replacement was an option, she was petitioning the state for euthanasia, if you can believe it."

I could. When I was 16 I shaved off my eyebrows and walked into traffic. In the hospital, the nurse asked me if I was having a nervous breakdown. I think I tried to quote "Lady Lazarus," but she didn't get the reference.

The night of the party, I got to Moira's first, early enough to watch her fret and fuss over the lighting, the mood, arranging and rearranging the chairs along the walls to leave room for dancing, if people wanted to. She kept adding rum to the punch bowl and making me take sips from the crystal ladle, lifting it to my mouth. "Is it better now? How about now?"

Moira threw good parties. She moved in a lot of circles, knew a lot of nubile young things with great shoulders. She worked on film sets downtown, wrangling extras or ushering celebrities from trailer to set. She did well in that environment. Moira and the men. She worked on big movies. She'd actually seen Leonardo DiCaprio's butt once. She said it aged him. *Nothing from the '90s is still beautiful.*

Moira appreciated ambiance, she understood good and bad vibes. She tuned the dimmer for the kitchen light until it was just right, and the room was cast in a warm, amber glow. We were ready for guests.

They started to arrive, first some women from Moira's yoga teaching days – two witchy types with long bell sleeves and their hair wound up in silk scarves. They each kissed Moira on the mouth and then lit up a joint, settling themselves at the kitchen table. Moira poured two cups of rum punch, garnishing them with orange slices. The witches drank and smoked, and one of them offered me the joint, but I shook my head. Moira topped up my club soda with a disapproving look. It was important that I didn't get fucked up at parties. Whenever I did, I got prickly, volatile, like a fox caught in a trap. If someone grabbed my arm for support, doubled over and laughing at a joke, I'd scratch their face.

A group of girls trickled in, young things from one of Moira's weekend groups for running in the park or extreme frisbee. Then some guys arrived with a two-four and at once, as was the case with good parties, the apartment erupted in noise. Moira sank into a chair in the living room and let herself relax; forgetting about me, and my problem, and the purpose of the party. She took a drag of some guy's vape and argued jovially with him over a director's lack of people skills. More people arrived. The yoga witches were stoned and giggling, tearing into bags of saltines they'd excavated from Moira's cupboards. She never had real food, mostly condiments, tomato soup, and cocktail fixings.

I stayed in the kitchen and shifted myself up to sit up on the counter. I could see the whole apartment from there. It was modern, open concept – Moira did well financially, set jobs were lucrative if you could stand the long hours – and for a while I made small talk with people as they passed by: *How do you know Moira? Was Leo an asshole on set?* Then I was alone for a bit too long, surveying the fluid movement of bodies in and out of the kitchen, from the punch bowl to the fridge to the long green velvet couch. In a crowd, bodies moved like liquid. You could be lifted off your feet and carried across a stadium before getting crushed up against a concrete wall. Death by crushing meant suffocation. I couldn't remember where I'd read that, but it felt important and then it felt dangerous. My vision swam white for a second, and I realized I was holding my breath.

I closed my eyes and tried to calm down, tried to remember what the therapist told me to do when my mind played violent tricks on me. I hated the therapist's office. There weren't any windows, and the furniture was too soft. She made you take off your shoes before you came in. *Stay grounded. Root yourself. Feel where your body makes contact with the world around you.* That never worked. When I felt my socked feet on the floor or my body against the couch, I panicked. It wasn't good for me, to be too aware of my body. Because then I'd feel the area. The way it had been looked at. Like a secret I'd been told about but couldn't understand. My cousin bent over and leaning down to hold up my skirt. He was much bigger than me. I could see the blond hair on his forearms, like desert shrubs in miniature, caught in the morning light.

"Hey," Moira said. I opened my eyes. She was standing in front of me, grinning, her eyes milky and red. She was stoned. "Don't be alone. Come sit with me." She grabbed my hand and pulled me off the counter and out of the kitchen. I was grateful for Moira. She was speedy, insistent. Pot always made her hyper. She tugged me through the party and the room was a rush of colour and skin. I forgot about my body.

She settled me on the couch beside two people who were deep in conversation. Moira sat in front of us on the floor, legs crossed. Her attention was fixed on the woman.

"This is Mark, Becca," she rattled off their names and pointed to each face. They looked over at me. Becca smiled and Mark gave a little wave, registering my arrival, before turning back to each other.

"The thing I still don't get is why people feel like they need it?" Mark said. He was the guy with the vape Moira had been talking to earlier. He was wearing a black ball cap and shorts.

"Well, for me," Becca said, touching her hand to her chest. "And I can't speak for other people, but I always knew I wanted it gone."

They were talking about operations, replacements, like the one I was going to get. I glanced at Moira. She was grinning the way she did when she was excited about meeting someone new. She was crushing on Becca, experiencing the pink gooey distraction I'd never fully known. I'd only seen it in other people.

Becca's hand moved from her chest to tug the lobe of her right ear, the one facing me on the couch and, in the half light of Moira's mood lighting, I could see the ear was a replacement. It was beautiful. The surgeon had done an excellent job. It was soft to her touch, flexible, but a natural shade of very pale green. The kind of green you might see outside in a tree but have a hard time finding anywhere else.

"What material did you choose?" I asked.

"Silicone," Becca said. She let go of her earlobe. "Silica is biodegradable so it will actually break up with my body. When I die. That's why I chose it."

"That's beautiful," Moira oozed and touched Becca's knee. Becca smiled down at her.

"Thanks."

"You get to choose the material?" Mark asked from Becca's other side on the couch.

"Of course," Becca said. "That's kind of the whole point. The redefinition."

"But *why* your ear?"

"I wanted it gone."

"So why not a reconstruction? Why not plastic surgery?"

Becca smiled. "You either want it or you don't. I didn't want to make do with my ear; I didn't want a different ear made up from the one I already had. I wanted to cut it off. I didn't want to feel that ear anymore."

"She's getting a replacement, too," Moira said nodding at me.

It took her a slow, stoned second to realize she'd revealed my secret. At first, she was looking at Becca and then she was turning to me, her mouth open.

"I'm sorry," she said.

"It's fine," I waved it off, casual.

"You are?" Becca leaned towards me. "You're getting your ear replaced?"

"No," I shook my head. "Well, yes, I'm getting a replacement. But not my ear. In a couple of weeks."

"Where?" Mark said, giving me the same horrified look Moira did in the bar, the up and down, calculating my parts, their weight.

"I'd rather not say." I blushed, and at the same time it occurred to Becca and Mark that my replacement might not be like other ones they'd seen. Not like the sculpted red shoulders and biceps they'd seen in the subway ads. Not like an ear.

"We're not supposed to ask, anyway," Becca said, trying to make me feel better. "It's private."

She slipped her foot into Moira's lap, acknowledging Moira's affection, reciprocating it. *You can touch me if you want.* Moira picked up the foot like she'd been given something precious to take care of. She stroked it.

"You're not doing a breast are you?" Mark said.

"It's private," Becca repeated.

"It's not her boobs," Moira said, forlorn, still stroking Becca's foot. Nothing could cheer her up on the subject of my replacement.

Mark shook his head at me.

"You're beautiful, what could you want to cut off?"

For a second, with the three of them staring at me, I wanted to be understood. I wanted to explain, it wasn't that there was anything wrong with the way I'd been born. The problem was how I'd been used, like an instrument bent and played the wrong way, upside down. Surely, they could understand?

Mark drained a beer and his Adam's apple rose and fell, rose and fell. I wanted to pinch it in my fingers and squeeze it until it popped. I'd never felt gooey, but I knew violence, the desire to interfere with the course of another person's night. Becca steered the conversation expertly to milder topics, a band she'd seen play down at the waterfront the weekend before. Mark watched me. In the end, I went home with him. Maybe to prove a point. To who, I wasn't sure.

"You're beautiful," he told me in the dark before he took off my clothes. He touched me like it was his duty to make me whole person. *You might not want to be touched,* the trauma therapist said over and over. *And that's okay.* The truth was I never minded the touching. I was used to it. With his finger on the button between my legs, he said: "You're beautiful, you're beautiful," again and again, and I thought of a quote I'd read or heard once but couldn't remember where. *What a waste beauty is, never to be enjoyed.* I was never very good at remembering where quotes came from.

I let him fuck me because it was the last time and because fucking, for me, was more like dying anyway. In the end, I got to be reborn. It was like a bad smell in the back of a mouth that could only mean aging, decay, time catching up with skin, and spit, and sweat. I remembered all the specifics of being a child, smashing Barbies together naked, their stiff arms extended out like they yearned to bend, to flex and become soft. I remembered the promise of a surprise I'd get later, after school, if I was a good girl. And if I wasn't, the threat of a broom handle, put inside a place, a hole inside me that I didn't even know existed. Then, the urgent touch and how it froze me, stopped everything silent, and how colour and sound didn't make sense anymore. How could the ceiling over the bed be purple? It had always been white.

When Mark was finished, and it was over; I got to be alive again. And I imagined the instrument between my legs melting into something that couldn't feel. Something flat, smooth, and simple. Something I got to put down and forget about. Something plastic.

Kate Felix-Segriff

THE POET OF BLIND RIVER

It was 1999 when you came to me, Jimmy.

I was on a VIA train, 80 kilometres out from Pacific Central Station and caught up in a bit of a situation. The waves of that situation were coming on strong but, instead of slipping beneath the surface of it, my mind lowered its anchor, and what it began to circle around was you.

I had locked myself inside the washroom of the train, had already been in there for 20 minutes, and soon enough some asshole would come and hammer on the door to find out what the hell was going on. But right then, at the moment I thought of you, I was still safe, still crouched on the lid of the toilet, a plank-walker trying not to leap.

I rocked with the motion of the train and muttered the one thing I still remembered from rehab, the chant we were supposed to keep in our pocket for the end of the line, when we were just about to cave.

"I will not use for the next two minutes, and then I will decide."

Wait. Wait.

"I will not use for the next two minutes..."

And on it went until the asshole started banging.

I pressed my palms against my eyelids and the sudden rush of darkness made me think of a poem you had written back when we were 17 – something about a bird's wing beating in the night sky – and it was a terrible poem to be honest, all of them were, but still, the darkness made me think of it. The details eluded me, but I recalled the point of it had been that feeling you get when a whole lot of shit seems to be passing you by and you cannot catch a hold of any of it. I had known the poem was really about me – they all were, back then – and the thing we had always fought about: How I had never seemed to actually *feel* anything, at least not completely.

Should we really have been surprised that you never got anywhere with your poetry? I mean, how could you with such a shitty muse? Maybe the real question should have been why a couple of northern kids like us ever thought we should try to express ourselves in a complex way? Probably we should have just stuck to underage drinking and fucking in the back of a Honda.

The rush of my inevitable screaming match with the asshole in the bathroom was enough to grant me temporary reprieve from my craving, so I went back to my seat and had a look at the map in the seat pocket. The train was en route from Vancouver to Sudbury, and I was travelling on it to see about a job I had been offered in a marginal dog sled operation back home in Blind River.

I traced my finger over the names of the cities we would be stopping in, and when I got to Edmonton I paused. I remembered how you had moved out there after the break-up, and I started to wonder whether you might want to see me.

Part of me wanted to forget it because I had accumulated a lot of scars since I had last seen you. I had been a ripe fruit back when we had been together, but I had not been kind to myself in the four years we had put between us. I was aware that my rotten bits were starting to show, and I wanted to stay in your mind's eye as a force of the universe; the one who had peeled out of the Food City parking lot on Huron Avenue and laughed while you had chucked all of your notebooks at the back of my Honda.

It felt good to think of you, Jimmy, like sucking on the hole of a missing tooth, and it went a long way to distracting me from my larger demons; the ones who told me to slip my fingers down into my pocket and caress the edges of the orange plastic container that was nestled there like a newborn kitten.

I looked up from the map and tried to watch the scenery as it whipped by the window. We were somewhere around North Bend, had just passed over the Fraser River, and I tried to focus on the Rocky Mountains as they started to appear. I thought about how I was supposed to be "reconnecting with the beauty of the world," as my sister had advised. She had paid for my ticket, saying all those white peaks and blue sky would be just the thing to "snap me out of my funk."

You will recall that was something I had never been able to stand about my sister – her sickening optimism. Her solution for malignant depression? A nice, hot bath. Life falling apart at the seams? Make a list. I realize it was kind of a screwed-up thing to dislike about someone, but back then I spent most of my time standing in a hailstorm, all of that sunshine was really starting to burn up my eyes.

That was the thing I had always liked about us, Jimmy: the way we never felt guilty about how we acted. When we fought it was brutal, but in a way it was also a thing of beauty. Holding it all in is killer sometimes, all that watching your words and trying not to act too feral, but that was never an issue with you and me. Once we got to howling, we would just keep at it until our throats were worn raw, but at the end of it all we always came out feeling clean.

I remembered how when we were done scrapping, we would just lay down beside each other and wait for our breath to settle; how sometimes you would reach out your hand and we would just hang there while it all washed over us. I thought of how afterwards we would take the Honda and park it out on the sideroad and you would grind yourself into me, like you were desperate to pin me down in that moment between pain and pleasure. I loved the way your voice got choppy right before you came, and how when you did, you would cry out like you were almost surprised by it, like the sweetness just crept out of nowhere and bit you.

Remembering all of that made me think I should not call you, that I had done a pretty solid job of tearing out your insides before I had left for Vancouver, and the humane thing might be to just let you lie. But you know better than anyone how I have always been disinclined to leave well enough alone, so as the train lurched eastward toward the interior, I started wondering how I could get your number.

I had given up looking at the mountains by then. It felt like they were mocking me, like they knew how goddamn beautiful they were and just wanted to throw it in my face. I thought about how their luminous peaks might disappear entirely, if I just let myself take a few hits from my orange container. I knew from experience, though, that once I started thinking down that path, the slope got steep pretty quick, so I started to look around for someplace else to put my mind.

The lady beside me was rummaging through her purse, and when she pulled out a cell phone, I found my new focus. Not everyone had a cell back then, so I started asking her about how it worked. She was pretty okay with me at first, but after a while she got freaked out by my pressured inquiries. The thing was, I could not shut up because, by that point, that lady and her goddamn phone were the only things standing between myself and another trip to the washroom.

I asked her if I could use the phone to call up somebody I needed reach in Blind River. She was not too keen, but my powers of negotiation were pretty rock-solid after three straight years of haunting emergency departments looking for Percocet scripts. Eventually, she just sighed and handed it over.

I could not quite recall your old number, but my fingers knew the pattern on the keypad from dialling it a hundred times a day back when I was 17. As it started to ring, I made a deal with the universe. I told it if the number was right, I would put the pills back in my suitcase until at least Jasper. I made a lot of decisions like that back then, by just holding my breath and waiting for the universe to decide if it was going to throw me a bone or just pull out the fucking rug.

Your mom answered on the second ring and she spoke to me like she was punched-up drunk to hear from me, like the break-up and all that ugliness after it had never happened and I was just one of her old gal pals. I thought of her standing there in your old kitchen, winding that pink phone cord through her fingers while she shot the shit, and I wondered what it would be like to be her – to be that ordinary – for just for one minute.

She launched into that story that always drove you buck-wild, the one about how your creeper dad had been driving a streetcar through Toronto back in the 70s. Your mom had been his last passenger at the end of the line and she told me how, deep in the middle of that rainy night, old Barry had shut the streetcar's doors tight and refused to let her off until she gave him her number. She had not liked the look of him – who could blame her? – so she had just sat there and watched as the drops streaked down the windows for the better part of 20 minutes. Then desperation had gotten the better of her, and she had relented.

She loved that story more than anything, and even though I could not see her, I knew she was smiling like a cat in a sunbaked window as she told it. I have always admired your mom's ability to weave a tender love story out of the fact that your dad had basically held her hostage on public transit.

I'm not sure why I cut her more slack than my sister. Maybe I liked the fact that your mom paid the price for her romantic notions and got to ride that sweet delusion through 25 years of a shitty marriage and three out-of-control kids. There were a lot of things in my own life that might have been easier to stand if I had only had her ability to ignore the parts of my story that did not fit with the overall vision.

Right before we rang off, she gave me your new number and said, "Good luck, honey. I hope you manage to reach our Jimbo," and I almost choked up because, at that point in my life, I was no longer used to such uncomplicated encouragement.

I did not feel like having a Courtney Love moment right there in plain view of my seatmates, so I pushed past the phone-lady and headed down to the luggage zone to pay my dues to the universe. The lady got up from her seat and started to chase me down the aisle yelling, "Hey-hey-hey." I realized I had forgotten to give her back the phone, so I thrust it backwards, told her to fucking relax, and carried on down the aisle.

As I locked my little bitches up in my suitcase, I thought about how my life might have been different if I had been able to get a more solid grip on things; how, if I had never broken my hand and discovered Percocet, we might have been able to skip the whole scene at Food City. Maybe you would never have written me that poem called "Go Fuck Yourself." Maybe instead we would have been living in some shit-box out on Michigan Avenue with a couple of kids, and I would be giving you grief for spending all your afternoons upside-down and waist-deep in some broken engine while those kids screamed circles around my ankles and drove me crazy. I considered how everything had turned out, on my end anyways, and I decided that life might not have been so terrible.

When I got back to my seat, my seatmate was gone and so was all of her stuff, so I was alone for the 10 hours it took us to get to Jasper. Sleep eluded me, so I sat there fidgeting and measuring the hours in two-minute intervals. I tried to break things up a little by looking out the window, but there was nothing to see beyond all of that night. I thought about the Rockies and how they were all still out there, even though they were invisible. I thought of their ancient origins and my own impermanence and all of that cliché shit people think about when they are near to mountains, and as the train cut through the thick of the interior I started to enjoy the feeling of being surrounded.

I got to thinking about that night we had fallen asleep naked in your basement after we had finished screwing because we were still only 16 and had had that tiredness of little kids upon us. I remembered how somewhere in the early morning, Booze-Hound Barry had come to stand at the bottom of the steps, and you and I had pretended to still be sleeping while he had hovered there and watched us like the creep that he was. I guess we should have been scared, lying there exposed like that, but I think we had not been because we had both known that together we could have kicked his ass if it had come down to it.

All of that nostalgia must have knocked me out cold because the next thing I remember we were pulling into Jasper station.

There was a payphone right on the platform, and the skin on the back of my hand where I had written your number was starting to burn, but when I disembarked the train, I blew right past that phone and cut a straight path to the washroom.

The thing was, when I got so close to calling you, I lost my nerve. The way we had left things had not really seemed open to a reconciliation, and I was afraid all the bullshit that had happened to me in the interim might have left me too damaged to stand your ire.

I entered a stall, got up on the toilet lid, and closed my eyes, but the sweet thoughts would not come. All I could think about was the Percocet and that moment when I had put it back into my pocket before leaving the train. I tried to do my chant, but the minutes were suddenly too long, so I took out the bottle and tried to crack open the seal. I could not get the bastard undone, and as I started to bang the lid against the side of the stall, I realized what was happening: the universe was cackling.

I bolted from the stall and pretty well ripped the receiver off of that platform payphone as I hammered in your number. I listened to the phone ring, and I dared that shit-for-brains universe to let you answer.

When I heard your voice, the words gummed up in my throat, and I just stood there like a dunce while I listened to your litany of hellos. It was not until you started screaming, "Who the fuck is this?" that I snapped back into gear and told you to just can it and get your ass over to meet me at Edmonton station.

Even though we had not spoken in four years, we just sort of picked up right where we had left off. You said you were just on your way to work, for fuck sake, and did I ever think of giving a person some goddamn notice? I could hear a dull thumping in the background and I knew you were whacking your palms against the sides of your thighs the way you had always done when you were pissed at me. Some old guy came up and started grabbing hold of my arm and yelling at me to get back on the train so I told him to piss off, but you thought I was talking to you. You started to get fired up and I kept telling you, "Shut the fuck up and let me talk – just shut the fuck up and let me talk…"

Then you told me to go fuck myself, and it was just like old times.

Once we were rolling on the train again, I thought about your break-up poem and a couple of the lines came back to me: "*You will bury me / but when I rise from my grave of shit / it will be middle finger first / pointing skyward / at you / my sweetheart.*" I thought of all the intricate drivel I had listened to in west-coast coffee shops, and how none of it been able to hold a candle to the raw honesty of "Go Fuck Yourself." Those lines had been the purest form of art; just a sloppy, burning hurt that oozed all over the page.

Even the sweet memory of your teenage rage could only hold me for so long, and I doubt even a minute passed before tiny bits of green pills started to drift across my mind. It occurred to me then that I might never be cured of my addiction, because it would always be there, waiting for me to claim it. Even if I left it for a day, a year, or even four, I would probably return to it eventually because that high seemed too sweet to give up forever. I pushed my thumb hard into the top of the bottle, but it held tight, and I decided to wait another two minutes, then another two, and so on and so on, until eventually, by some miracle, we reached Edmonton.

I had already told myself you would not be there. Why would you be? After the phone call, the Food City parking lot, after everything that had happened, and hadn't. But I still felt my heart quicken as I hopped off the train, so I made the universe one last deal: I told it to put you on that platform and if it did, I would throw my stash in the garbage before I got back on the train.

But you were not there.

I slipped out the side door of the station with the bottle rattling in my hand and marched out to the parking lot to find myself some privacy to get high. While I was crossing the pavement, I kept thinking about how it was going to mean three months of rehab down the shitter, but I did not care. I just did not care, but I *did* care, just a little; that little bit was enough to make me look back at the station one last time and there you were, sitting behind the wheel of your work van, staring your angry lightning rods at the arrivals door.

You big, dumb fuck, there you were.

The Percocets seemed to scream bloody murder as they ricocheted on the inside of the trash can. I walked around to the passenger side and just stood there. I waited for you to notice me, and as I did, something started warming me up from inside.

I thought about how you had come to the station even though you were mad at me, how in some way you must still be on my side, and for that one minute as I stood there and looked at you, I knew what it might feel like to be ordinary, to have things in life I could depend on.

You looked like a top-grade asshole as you scowled through your windshield at the exiting passengers, but I could see that kid behind your eyes, the one who had tried to write poems, the one who had tried to solve things, the one who had tried to find small pockets of happiness in this rotted-out world.

As the stream of people thinned from the arrivals door, I watched as disappointment started to creep around the edges of your eyes. That was when I started to bang on the hood of your van because more than anything at that moment, I wanted you to see me.

I do not think I even said hello before I stuck my tongue down your throat, and you kissed me back hard because I think we both knew that train would be leaving in 45 minutes, and it was the last stop for us; that after the universe paused for those brief moments, we would permanently travel in different directions and never crash into each other again.

***

It has been four years since they decided to rip up Queen Street, and as I stare down at the mess they have made beneath my apartment window, it occurs to me that they will never completely fix it. There is a construction guy pacing the ruptured sidewalk below as he screams obscenities into his cell phone and waves his tattooed arms through the steam of the afternoon. In a different life, I would have leaned across my sill and shouted down an invitation. But today, I think I will skip it.

I have been holding myself closer these days. I have been taking better care. Even my sister has started to come back around to a cautious hope that the seasons, for me, might be finally changing. So, instead of plunging down there into the heat and mess of the day, I will sit up here at my third-hand desk and think about all the shit that seems to have passed me by.

I picture you as you might look at this precise moment, perched atop some oil rig in the middle of a sand swamp. You have probably gotten paunchy from too many hours spent in a Fort Mac sports bar, swigging your beers and yelling your insults to a shiny big-screen. I imagine your eyes grown tired, and how your face must hang loose now, like mine. Forty-six years, Jimmy. Forty-six years of living on the edge of things.

Does that afternoon you met me at the Edmonton station ever cross your mind? As you try to ignore that last whisky in the mini-bar and spread yourself wide atop that pale-patterned comforter, do you ever look over at the identical bed beside you, and wonder what it would be like if that bed was occupied? If the universe had just thrown me down beside you, and let me stay?

I heard your mom moved in with your sister a few years ago, after your dad's accident. So even if my fingers still remembered your old number, that tap dance over the digits would only deliver me to somebody else's kitchen or the sound of a disconnected line.

And I'm proud to tell you, Jimmy, that I have finally learned a thing or two about leaving things be, so I will not even try, this time, to track you down.

But there are some things the universe wants you to know.

It wants you to know that I held on to those moments we stole together in the summer of '99; stored them inside myself for years afterwards, through all sorts of terrible shit you do not ever need to consider.

It wants you to know those brief moments of life in the train station parking lot gave me hope where I might otherwise have had none, and that sometimes, even the smallest shreds of hope can be braided together to form a rescue line.

It wants you to know that as all of those crates and tools smashed down around us in the back of your work van, I felt the molecules of my brain start to buzz, and finally, as I drove you inside of me, that I felt every inch of you.

For two sweet minutes.

Completely.

Linda Rogers

RAPUNZEL

It hurt like hell when Skip cut my braids off. I'm not kidding. Hair has feelings, just like carrots and elephants, who actually cry out loud, but Skip and my mother were oblivious to my pain. In the Skip moment, I found out some people have no nerve endings, their neurotransmitters snipped off, just like my long golden hair.

I loved my hair, loved the story of Rapunzel, which my brother read to me before I taught myself to compensate for our AWOL egg and sperm donors, who were too busy being a prince and princess themselves to weave fantasy gardens for kids.

Rapunzel grew her hair into a long rope that let her prince climb into the tower where she lived alone, reading comics, and eating ice cream delivered by good fairies at midnight. I had similar aspirations, and then, one summer day, Skip, the *au pair,* my mother's confidante, brought them crashing down.

We were having a grace and favour holiday, the guests of sympathetic friends who had a beach cottage and a wild Welsh mountain pony that resented adults much as I did. No one else could feed that pony apples without having their hand bitten off. No one else could get on her without being bucked off.

That was the summer I discovered it is harder to control a deranged mother than a willful horse. Some mothers cannot be charmed or distracted. Some mothers must be obeyed. Mine was on a mission and Skip was her besotted accomplice.

On the gender spectrum, I had been a restless nerd, a girl who needed books to devour and trees to climb, one who argued fiercely, and argued to win. I had been judged a tomboy who loved fern fights and playing horses with my friend, Madelyn – Mad for short – but wrong, I was all girl, planting my flag in no girls' land.

I had revelled in androgyny, *She for the Goddess only, He for the Goddess in her*, but my female parent had a new imperative. The needle had to move. She now required a male child. Not my decision. I mention this because someone, Skip, not my mother, who is now gaga, would argue that I had asked for the transformation.

Without notice, my Wettums doll was consigned to the nuisance ground. I was told her insides had rotted from constant feeding and she'd died in the doll hospital. My beautiful dresses, sent by an aunt whose obsessive need to smock held off alcoholism for a while, were donated to a thrift shop. I was given a holster with two cap pistols and permission to attend the cultural war in our lane – the annihilation of Indigenous surrogates.

Heretofore, my play persona had been Sacajawea, the brains of the Lewis and Clarke expeditions. I stood on the high rock in the Simpson boys' yard and argued for peace and reconciliation, my peace pipe filled with tobacco swiped from my father's pouch. In my new crew cut and khaki shorts, I transformed into Gene Autry, the crooning cowgirl. Until I started to go to Saturday matinees and saw him singing "Home on the Range," I'd identified with Gene, somewhere else on the spectrum.

Skip, our rescue nanny, was a former gang member. I gave her a wide berth. She was the egg donor's *au pair*, and I learned from my autodidact French study about Madame Sourire, a mouse that smiled, who should have meant an extra pair of hands to wash the dishes, and fold the laundry, not to pick up a pair of scissors and change my life. Again. Snip.

Skip was way farther down the androgyny road than I was, with her cropped hair and boy walk. My brother explained what that meant. He explained gaydom, told me he had sex feelings for boys. I didn't even know what sex feelings were, even after being accosted by a man without pants in the woods where we built forts and picked huckleberries; and the Mountie who came to interview me asked about certain words, which I denied knowing. Of course.

Realizing I needed to speak the language of jurisprudence, I upped my game, researched the proper names for a few body parts and helped put a couple of pervs in jail, but I still thought the whole crime was exposure, undressing in public and trying to convince little girls that the thingy dangling between their legs was a doll to play with. I knew dolls were inanimate, not dangly body parts. Dolls were for little girls, just as babies were for mums and *nannies*. Such was the child-received division of gender in those days and the rest of it was ether, non-empirical.

When our biology teacher told us the penis fit in the vagina like a hand in a glove, oh really? I was truly surprised.

We were free-range kids. The woods were not forbidden, an omission I now find strange, but such is the detachment of narcissistic parents. Details like safety hardly mattered, until they did.

Today, I watched a video of a toddler walking through an open gate in the fence around a swimming pool and, duh, tumbling in. The dad, known as Duh for the purpose of this retelling, told media after he saved the kid from drowning, "I'm going public so people will pay attention to pool safety." Oh, Duh, you bought a pool. Pools are not all Hockney paintings. Stupid Dad.

❧

The Big Change started with a family moment that led to my brother offering to trade his piggy bank for my skipping rope.

It was Sunday morning. Our parents were sleeping in. Normally we got ourselves up, poured cereal in a bowl, gobbled it, and left for Sunday school, where there was a heap of happy clapping and singing. We liked clapping and singing. We liked Jesus bidding us to shine. We liked the tender view of little sparrows and the fact that a man with a gentle face loved us unconditionally, his little lambs. No one else in our post-colonial world used endearments like that.

But this Sunday, we defaulted. There was an interval in a storm, both at home and outside, where the trees in our garden shook, dropping apples on the lawn, and it looked like more weather was coming. Why risk getting soaked even though not going to church would mean we were in for the big Sunday sulk, words unspoken, food untouched? We were used to fights, our parents accusing one another of high crimes and misdemeanours that ranged from adultery to hoarding mother's little helpers.

Both units needed to be the centre of attention. Both were the children of invalids. Our grandfather was defoliated in the war to end all wars (if only). Our grandmother had a broken heart and had given what was left of it to Jesus, none of it left for the attention-seeking soprano we called Mum. We knew our parents' narcissism grew out of their parents' hypochondriacal self-absorption, and we also knew that that was no excuse.

When I think about how my brother and I were made, I see two broken sticks rubbing together, trying to start a fire that would thaw our frozen parents. *Suttee*, our style.

Our mother's desire for attention made her competitive with women and girls. She had to be number one. She had to be prettier than other girls, smarter than other girls. Our dad used the same playbook on my brother, constantly demeaning my mother's little fairy boy. Dad had to be king, and no princes. And no hiding places.

In general, we regarded them as theatre. They fought, they pouted, and apparently they fucked. They moved on and so did we. Domestic bumps had very little consequence in the larger theatre of Cold War raging around us, duck and cover, the need for bomb shelters.

This time was different. A small incident with my brother escalated and they kept it going all night long, while we kids barricaded ourselves behind my bedroom door.

The next night our fun couple went on a date – a concert and dinner – and after making fudge with a "smash," somewhere between a dash and half a cup of crème de menthe, we settled into the Mother Closet and began our rituals. First, we sniffed everything – her suits and dresses, her fur jackets, even her shoes – smearing it all with our fudge fingers. It's amazing how intoxicating the smell of her perfume mixed with sweat could be. High on mother musk, we selected our wardrobe, usually by sticky touch, my brother and I both favouring velvety as opposed to silky. We used the thumb test, rubbing the fabric between our thumbs and pointing fingers while sucking the other thumb. Whatever gave us sex feelings, we chose.

He settled on black velvet with a pink silk rose at the bosom and I picked the green Empire dress, trees being my optimum refuge. I loved the empire waistline and long sweeping skirt that trailed behind, her peekaboo bosoms aloft. She used that one a lot for recitals. My strawberry blonde hair was long and straight, my brother's longish for a boy, dark auburn and wavy as an oil slick. He twisted mine in a low chignon and pinned it with diamanté bobby pins. I lacquered his flat and back, like Hilary Swank at the Oscars the year she won for *Boys Don't Cry*. We took our time with make-up and, when we were done, sat side by side at her dressing table, gazing into our matching blue-green eyes, admiring our work. "Gorgeous," I said. He really was.

That was when they came in. That's when it started.

"It's all your fault," our father accused our mother. "You baby him."

"No, she's to blame. She's a dominatrix," our mother accused me.

"You're hardly ever home." I countered lamely.

It escalated. Things got thrown. Broken. We longed for Skip even though neither of us liked her. She had the knack of keeping our mother in check. But Skip was at an all-nighter. Her team had won the softball tournament and she was weekending with her gang. All night long, my brother and I lay side by side in my bed, with my chest of drawers against the door, wondering what came next.

Just at civil dawn, as the sun slipped like a golden yolk past the horizon and began its ascent, my father's eyes landed on the Warhol silk screen of my mother, and, when he called it a name she didn't like, she took an axe to it. Then she chopped up the oil painting of my father by his best friend who died in the war.

Everything in our house was defined by the war, war as a noun and a verb. While my father watched, I assume in masochistic fascination, my mother then took the axe to their conjugal bed, which she threw out the window in little pieces. Luckily, we weren't lurking on the terrace below.

Not that it didn't land on us anyway.

I wondered if my father was next. Reallly, I didn't care so long as she didn't come after my brother and me.

Finally, without drawing blood, she put down her weapon of mass destruction and passed out on the floor beside him. I always thought they enjoyed the fights, and later came to think of them as foreplay. The problem is they didn't let us in on their little drama secret. We thought the battles were real and we took them seriously.

When silence descended, we moved the furniture, cracked open the door, and verified the ceasefire, then tiptoed out of our safe room and made ourselves breakfast, adding the crème de menthe to our cereal. Crème de menthe was our comfort protest, carefully rationed, the crystallized bottle at the back of the liquor cabinet lasting forever. We saved it for fights. We were the grown-ups, sophisticated, wise, and they were the children. Crème de menthe validated us, and mixing it with milk, like Beethoven, is not as loud as it sounds.

In lieu of heading straight for Sunday school, where we swallowed the gospel and really good breakfasts of pancakes and bacon, my brother went to his room and got his piggy bank. He was saving for the yellow brick road. I knew, based on experience, his midnight journeys were solo, that I would not be invited to join because our magical thinking took us in different directions, him to midnight and me to High Noon, the cowboy and Indian confrontations in our lane.

"Wanna trade?" he asked casually, holding out his pink pig, shaking it so I could hear it was full of coins.

"What for?" What did I have that could possibly match such a magnificent get?

"I want your skipping rope."

"My skipping rope. Are you kidding?"

"Nope. I want your skipping rope and all the rhymes that go with it." He said weird stuff like that. I wondered which ones he meant, really meant. "On a mountain stands a lady...." So far, so good. Boy-girl stuff. Romance.

"All she has is gold and silver." I get it. He's giving me his. "All she wants is a fine young man." (That was the existential question, I guess.)

"Okay," I said, and my visible friend, still wearing the velvet dress and high heels, took off across the street into the forest, swinging my skipping rope like a lariat.

"All the boys love Harriet," I sang. "Harriet's handy with a lariat / But Harriet doesn't wanna marry yet / She's having too much fun."

I was dying to run after him, but I knew he'd send me back. Besides, someone had to hold off the vigilantes.

Maybe, when my father was calling my brother names, he let him know it would be smart to be handy with a rope for skipping and tying knots, and tying girls up and branding them, which is more or less what happened to me. He was running away from home, something I dreamed about but, unlike him, never had the jam to carry out.

It looked like he was heading toward the fort in the woods where Mad and I played doctor. "No boys allowed," I yelled after him/her as he vanished with a smirk, a very credible girl in high heels and evening dress. "*Taa-rrra*," his raised middle finger disappeared in green like the Cheshire Cat's smile.

Whenever I think of him, I see that finger.

My brother stayed lost. I couldn't tell them where he had gone. I didn't know. That was his business. He left all the time, sometimes returned like a crow with small treasures – a kitten, or a rhinestone barrette he found on the sidewalk – and almost always a story. My brother frequented all-night diners and often came home smelling of ketchup. He always found a lonely person to buy him breakfast in exchange for hearing him out. Diners are great places for that.

⁂

They actually didn't notice until Monday.

"Why didn't you say anything?"

"Why would I? He takes off all the time."

"A whole day? What were you thinking?"

"I was thinking he took a holiday. Maybe he did. Like I said, he comes back. The cat comes back. You know the words." I knew she didn't. She could rattle off lyrics in a dozen languages, but kids' songs, songs her kids might like to sing with her? Not a hope in hell.

"What are you talking about? Where? Is? He?"

"I! Don't! Know!" She was rough, pinching my shoulders. I was crying by then. They would have to bite the bullet and call the cops, again. That was embarrassing, wouldn't look good on her résumé and, besides, my bro was her little man.

My dad was beyond irritated with all of us. Me. Her. My brother. We were inconveniencing him. He had meetings to attend.

The cops turned up with my skipping rope. It took them two days, but they found it tied to a branch on a tall skinny tree that had fallen over.

"Is this your rope?"

"Looks like it."

"What did he tell you?"

"Nothing."

"Where is he?"

Even at nine, I was a big fiction reader. "The fairies probably took him. I think he was hoping for that."

"Do fairies make nooses?" the cop asked.

"All the time when they're hunting for teeth."

"Stop it!" I thought my dad was going to hit me.

"Maybe a wild animal ate him,"mother moaned, "and it's..."

"All her fault," I finished the sentence with her, the first of more times than you can count on a centipede's toes, not even counting when she'd already accused me of brewing the elixir that had made him light in his loafers.

"She's right," I said. "It was a unicorn."

I had to get the cops on side, make them see this was a family any red-blooded fairy would run from.

"We have a missing boy and a rope," one big guy said while the other two looked at their shoes. "No note, no clues from his sister, and no body."

The case stayed open, and my parents behaved as if he was dead. I knew he wasn't. He didn't feel dead, just missing in action, a 14-year-old on the lam. He hadn't acted as if he wanted to be dead. Sure, he gave me his piggy bank, but I knew that was just a red herring. When I dumped it out, there was only small change adding up to about $60. My brother was a miser, and I knew he had a fortune in birthday money stashed somewhere else, enough to get to an all-night diner where no one would know him and some sugar daddy was waiting to tell him a sad story that never ended.

I pissed his change away on comics and jawbreakers.

Skip cut my braids off, and my mother made me dress like a boy. But it wasn't the end of the world. My hair would grow. I would outgrow my brother's name and his clothes. My mother would outgrow her voice and settle down at home. She would try to seduce me as she had him, and I would punch her so hard she would roll out of my bed and bang her head on the floor. My father would get caught penetrating a dancer, and my mother would get dementia, also my fault because of the bed incident. All this would happen. "Suck it up, Princess," I told myself. "The cat came back."

That never happened, but I grew up, ditched the boy paraphernalia and the boy name, moved to Victoria, went to art school, and made bronze jewellery that looked like vines from the Garden of Eden but tied like nooses, no clasps just loops. When it started to sell, because, I assume, lots of people have living rope memories, unbiblical cords to untangle, I brandished his name or a version of it, back to the garden Eve, who made Eve Jewellery.

I made restaurant reservations under Eve, and my new friends called me Eve. I was a survivor. My brother had disappeared, not a clue anywhere even though I asked around and searched the internet.

On a sales visit to Vancouver, I called my mother and Skip answered the phone. "We're married now," she said, "And you don't exist."

"Way to go, Skip, from *au pair* to heiress," I said and hung up.

I took a cab and cruised by the old house, saw an old lady in a wheelchair on the terrace and asked the driver to stop. While he waited, I took out the elastics holding my braids, shook my hair and walked up the driveway. The sun was behind me. I knew my red-gold hair shone like her rising son. The old lady stared at me gape-mouthed, as if I was a rare bird she'd spotted in the shrubs.

"What's your name?" she said.

"Rapunzel." I laughed, maybe manically. Some of us don't know how to control our voices.

"You're trespassing, Rapunzel."

I picked a rose on my way out.

"He killed a tree," the old lady shouted as I got in my cab. I didn't look back.

❧

The jewellery show was at the Georgia Hotel. I decided to pop into the beauty salon and have my hair done. The salon was crowded, but I was lucky, someone had cancelled. The stylist took me to her chair and felt my hair.

"I'm Eve. What can I do for you? Shampoo? Cut?"

"I'm Eve too, and I just want a set. I braided it so it would crimp. My hair is straight."

"I wish," the hairdresser said. "The grass is always greener."

I looked at her hair. Very curly, shaved on one side and teased on top, auburn as a chestnut pony.

"We could trade."

"My sister used to say that."

"Pots," I said.

"Pans," she answered.

"Pins."

"Needles."

We laughed.

"I make jewellery and I'm modelling it tonight. Could you put my hair up and work some of this into it?" I opened my bag and pulled out my Sisyphus tiara, a couple of clips, and a necklace to weave into a chignon.

"Wow," she said. "Lots to work with."

"Oh, I have a warehouse full."

"No, I mean your hair."

"I haven't cut it since I left home."

"Home?"

"It's a long story."

She got to work pinning up my hair and spraying it in place. I kept my eyes shut until she was done. I wanted the full surprise. Then she held a hand mirror and swung my chair around.

"Take a look! You look gorgeous," she said, and I met her green eyes in the mirror. She looked away, just for the bat of a false eyelash, and I knew not just one but two strong women had survived the family gender wars.

"Not as gorgeous as you, Evan. Never."

Darlene Madott

NEWTON'S LAW

For every action there is an equal and opposite reaction

Mrs. Iryna Buriak receives her mother's inheritance and uses it not to pay down a mortgage that collaterally secures Mr. Buriak's monument business, but to secretly retain a divorce lawyer.

Thirty-five years ago, at the age of twenty, she had started in the monument business as a receptionist working for Mr. Buriak, Senior. Iryna had been beautiful, then – fulsome, blonde, her face as yet untouched by cigarettes, alcohol, or Mr. Bohdan Buriak, Junior. She continued on as a receptionist after marriage at the age of twenty-two to the boss's son, through two children and thirty-three years of marriage.

Because of Mrs. Iryna Buriak's stubborn refusal to use her inheritance from her late mother to pay down his business mortgage, Mr. Bohdan Buriak sends his wife into the cold storage room where the monuments are kept, to take inventory. Cold storage is where Mr. Bohdan Buriak always sends Mrs. Iryna Buriak to punish her. Cold storage after she bought a Christmas tablecloth. Cold storage after she purchased winter boots for their youngest son – Yurij had outgrown his boots before the Boxing Day sales before Ukrainian Christmas, and Mrs. Iryna Buriak didn't think the child should struggle through snow in boots two sizes too small. Cold storage for *not* buying day-old bread...

After two weeks of taking inventory of the marble headstones and plaques, now fifty-five years of age, Mrs. Iryna Buriak contracts bronchitis, but recovers quickly.

Mrs. Iryna Buriak goes to the Buduchnist Credit Union and withdraws her inheritance.

Mrs. Iryna Buriak's lawyer sends a letter announcing her client's desire to separate "as amicably and as respectfully as possible." Upon receiving it, Mr. Bohdan Buriak has his bookkeeper send his wife a letter terminating her employment. Her termination is for "unspecified cause." He does not pay the minimum severance required by the Employment Standards Act.

She takes her first day off work in thirty-five years, not counting the days following the birth of each of their two sons, Danylo Buriak, now nineteen and Yurij Buriak, now eleven. The youngest, Yurij, was a surprise, born to Mrs. Iryna Buriak in her forty-fourth year.

On her first day off work, Mrs. Iryna Buriak removes Mr. Bohdan Buriak's coin collection from the lower drawers of the armoire in the matrimonial bedroom. She drives north to visit a loyal cousin, Michael Morozenko. Together, they photograph each of the coins. She leaves the coins in Michael Morozenko's cellar, for safe keeping. The photos are sent to a coin specialist, for valuation. She tells the specialist to be on particular lookout for a Ukranian coin that first landed on Canadian soil in the heel of Mr. Buriak, Senior's boot.

Mrs. Iryna Buriak's lawyer writes a second letter, advising the coins have been removed to safe keeping and for valuation, while urging Mr. Bohdan Buriak to retain counsel and to reinstate his wife's salary.

Mr. Bohdan Buriak refuses to hire counsel. He refuses to reinstate his wife's salary.

Mr. Bohdan Buriak threatens the wife's counsel with criminal charges for harbouring "stolen goods." He is certain his wife's lawyer has his coins.

Mrs. Iryna Buriak commences an Application for Divorce.

Their first time in court, Mrs. Iryna Buriak passes the hours waiting for the case to be called by doing her needlepoint. Patiently, she stitches beautifully coloured letters onto a pillow, as if she were brushing colours onto a Ukrainian Easter egg, each stitch a needle into a Voodoo doll: "Don't Dare Sleep." She will leave the pillow on Mr. Bohdan Buriak's side of the bed.

Mr. Bohdan Buriak refuses to leave the matrimonial home. He will not co-operate in a joint listing of the property. A motion will have to be brought for its sale.

Mr. Bohdan Buriak will insist upon his own real estate agent.

He will take down the signs of *her* real estate agent, hide these behind the enormous obstructing trunk of the grand maple tree in the backyard.

Mrs. Iryna Buriak goes grocery shopping. In a frenzy of hammering, measuring, sawing, he constructs drywall down the centre of the home. She returns home with bags of groceries, only to find upon opening the front door that she must turn this way or that to enter from the right or the left half of the front entrance. Upstairs, she sees her husband has mounted the drywall up and over the matrimonial bed, such that it is impossible for either to get a proper sleep or to change the sheets.

Yet another motion is brought, to compel Mr. Bohdan Buriak to remove the drywall and to vacate the home, pending its sale. He is ordered to pay Mrs. Iryna Buriak's costs.

Mr. Bohdan Buriak goes to live with his elderly father, and from his new perch in the Buriak paternal home, Mr. Bohdan

Buriak continues to harass, to the point of terror, Mrs. Iryna Buriak.

The next motion is for Court approval to a *bona fide* third-party purchase offer to the house, for which Mr. Bohdan Buriak is unreasonably withholding his consent. At the eleventh hour, he relents and permits the offer.

The purchase price drops, after Mr. Bohdan Buriak contacts the prospective purchaser and warns of mould in the bathroom off the master bedroom.

Another motion is brought, to make the diminution of sale price between the first and second offer come out of Mr. Bohdan Buriak's notional half proceeds of sale, and to find Mr. Bohdan Buriak in contempt of court. The contempt motion is denied, for now, with a hefty admonishment. Mr. Bohdan Buriak is again ordered to pay the wife's costs.

"The Karma bus just left and he's not on it," Mrs. Iryna Buriak says to her lawyer, as she watches Mr. Bohdan Buriak leave the courtroom that day. "I almost feel sorry for him. No, I don't feel sorry for him. Maybe someday I will."

Action and Reaction

I, Iryna Buriak, *make oath and say as follows...* To hell with the affidavit format. Been there. Done that. I'm taking control of my own story. When you see the "I" it is me, Iryna, doing the telling. Doesn't matter to whom. Just assume it's to you. Just know it's the truth. This is my story:

I went to see a lawyer first. Then, my lawyer sent me off to do some homework. Tax bill, utility bills, try to figure out expenses toward figuring out property division. When I started looking for the paperwork, I realized it was all gone. Bohdan is an anal record keeper, and everything was gone. I think he has a plan. He hasn't actually gone to a lawyer, yet. But he is *preparing* to do something.

The day he got the letter of intent to separate was the day I removed the coins.

Bohdan sent me into cold storage.

I got bronchitis again.

He fired me.

He got served that afternoon.

My lawyer got an emergency hearing, on a cancellation, three days later. His lawyer couldn't figure out how we got to court so fast. Served on a Monday and we were in court on Thursday.

Bohdan wanted to change the date of separation to say we'd separated ten years earlier, so my claim to an equal share of everything would be out of time. You'd think his lawyer would have said something about how stupid that made him look, with Yurij age eleven, but no, he had to hear it from the judge.

The judge requested a meeting with the two lawyers in chambers. My lawyer told me over lunch what the judge had said. We were sitting in a Chinese restaurant, after court, and I was cackling hard at how the judge had summed up Bohdan – "Another Ukrainian guy with a God complex."

I wonder if the judge knew the history? Ukraine, the victim nation – bullied by Russia, Germany, Poland. There is something to be said for the inflated ego of survivors. My cousin Michael Morozenko thinks we're a pack of losers, always on the losing side of history.

The judge told both lawyers he'd had one of these Ukrainian guys in his first year of practice – a husband who'd had a bunch of his drunk Bohunk buddies over to the home while his wife was out, and damned if they didn't put up drywall right down the centre of the house. "It must be a Ukrainian thing," he said, because he'd never thought he'd live to see that one again.

The Squeaky Floor

My late mother had a twisted, wicked sense of humour. I must have inherited it. Never malicious. When Bohdan moved to the basement, in the period before the judge ordered him out, Bohdan built himself this lovely room that was fully finished. He'd go there to sleep. He is a very light sleeper. So, at night, I would set my alarm for two o'clock in the morning, to go outside and have a cigarette. I would creep back into the house. There was one spot in the hall. The floor creaked horribly.

I would stand in the hallway, exactly where the creaks were, and go *squeaky squeaky*, until I saw the light go on downstairs, and I'd creep back into my room and go back to sleep and he'd be up all night. Something my late mother would do. I swear, she must have been whispering in my ears, *Squeak the floors.*

I don't think he ever figured it out.

Wake him up, wake him up, wake him up.

That was my big retaliation. Didn't cost me anything. Didn't hurt anybody...

Two years, every night. *Squeaky, squeaky, squeaky, wake him up, wake him up, wake him up.*

And I was always able to go back to sleep, completely refreshed in the morning, dreams of the peace that comes from further vengeance dancing in my head.

I think that's when Bohdan went to the doctor and got sedatives.

Random Acts of Harmless Revenge

Before I gave him back all the keys to the company cars, I would, every now and then, randomly set off car alarms.

Bohdan would be getting his key into the front door, and off the cars would go, and he'd have to run down the drive to figure out what was going on.

After I bought my new car, from the costs the judge ordered against Mr. Buriak, I left the company keys on the kitchen table.

My Mother's Contents

Momma had died the year before I started the divorce proceedings and I had boxes of her stuff stored in the basement. Her stuff had been there for a couple of years. That's when, all of a sudden, things started to disappear from the home. I wasn't really aware of it. I happened to go down to do laundry, and as I was turning, I saw, *what's missing*? I started to go through the boxes. All the framed photos of me and my kids – all gone. Now I have no pictures of me with Danylo and Yurij. I was usually the one taking photos at family events. I was rarely *in* a picture with the kids. Now I have no pictures, at all.

It was like he wanted my actual life to have never existed. Gone. Disposed of.

I had a sentimental attachment to some of my Momma's stuff that I took with me after she died. There was a little antique dresser, with a swivel mirror, that was my grandmother's – *poof*, gone. I began doing the laundry again. There was this box on the workbench. I labelled all my boxes when I was moving. I turned around and it was labelled with the contents he had put in there – "old iron." *Where's my iron* – what old iron? I removed the tape carefully and it was this old cast-iron press that they had put hot coals into back in the Ukraine – they were my Baba's irons. And my Baba's old hand sickle brought from Ukraine. I took the sickle out of the box. There were all kinds of jars of screws and nuts and bolts lying around. Kind of weighed the sickle against them. Replaced Baba's irons and sickle with jars of screws. Re-taped the whole box and left it alone.

I started to go through the house. One day while he was at work, I lifted all the artwork off the walls, put it all in my car and drove it to my girlfriend's. It was stuff we had collected together, stuff that had really spoken to me when we'd bought it and hung it. He doesn't care about art, only its monetary value.

Appendix: The Useless Organ That Kills

"Momma, I don't feel good." It was just after Ukrainian Christmas. "Ah, you just ate too much crap. Did you go to the bathroom? Well, go to sleep. If you need me, come into the bedroom, you know where I am."

About two o'clock in the morning, I heard Yurij in the bathroom, throwing up. Yurij was about twelve or thirteen years old at the time.

I rinsed Yurij's mouth. I washed Yurij's face. I wondered if he will lie down.

"Momma, can I come in and lie down with you?" I thought, *Something is really wrong.* He was hot. At one point, "I feel better now, I'm going to go back to bed."

When I woke him up in the morning, he was on fire. He rolled over and moaned at me. "My stomach."

"Lie down on your back, show me where. Lower right quadrant? Get dressed, I'm going to take you to urgent care."

Doctor examined him, hit the spot, kid jackknifed. Had ultrasound. I ran outside to phone his father to let him know what's happening.

"Chances are he has appendicitis."

"I could have told you."

So the kid suffered all night, because his father wouldn't tell me what he knew to be true in his heart.

Once we got into the room, I gave his father a call and gave him the room number. He asked to speak to Yurij. Yurij was going to be taken for surgery within the next half hour.

"So, is your dad coming?"

"No, he's not coming. He told me he's not coming because you're here."

I don't get the games people play through the kids, to make each other miserable. But this was different. This was Mr. Bohdan Buriak not even wanting to see his youngest son, before surgery.

Acorns don't fall too far from the tree

Yurij's grandfather, Mr. Buriak, Senior, called me out of the blue.

"Is Yurij home?"

"No, he's out with friends."

"Well, I'd like to see him."

"Well, you'll have to speak to him. It's not up to me anymore."

"I'm going to come by your place."

"No, you're not. I'd prefer you didn't."

"It's not nice, Yurij doesn't return my calls. His own grandfather."

"Well, really, it's up to Yurij. All I can do is relay the message and encourage him."

"I'd like to stop by."

"As I said before, I'd prefer that you didn't."

"Yurij should be able to say who he sees."

"No doubt. However, it won't be here."

"I haven't talked to my grandson in a long time. We don't know if you're keeping him from us."

"Hold it right there. First of all, the boy is almost nineteen years old. I don't have much control over who he sees or doesn't. He's able to make his own choices. At this point, he chooses not to see you. I can't change his mind. And I'm not prepared to try to change his mind. It comes full circle."

"I don't know what happened to your marriage with Bohdan."

"Interesting, because when I took steps to try to talk to you, you took a different approach. You surgically removed me from the family."

"Bohdan and I, we don't talk anymore."

"That's too bad, because you're father and son."

"I don't know what happened. Bohdan doesn't talk to us."

"Again, not my problem."

Then, I took pity on the old man. I could see his big, red, perplexed face.

"Did you ever try *listening?*

Dead silence.

"Well, I'd still like to talk to Yurij."

Newton's Law for Ukrainians

For every action there is an equal and opposite reaction, except in the case of the Ukrainian male. The action is like running into a monument stone – absolutely immovable.

The Coin Return

The closing ceremony reflects the opening, which was the taking of the coins.

Our lawyers are in place. Except Bohdan's lawyer has, inexplicably, sent one of his young law clerks. Bohdan doesn't seem to care. He is too busy hating my lawyer.

So, it starts. This is the deal. What the lawyers have worked out. I have to give back all the coins and he is going to verify that each and every one is there. Out comes a coin. The coin is located on page thirty-six of the list. Bohdan turns each coin upside down, backwards and forward, and slowly acknowledges receipt.

Out comes the next coin. Same process.

There are coins he comments upon – like the coin from 1978 – that was a "very bad year. A disaster of a year." The young clerk asks, "Oh, Mr. Buriak, what made that a bad year?"

My lawyer answers, "It was the year they got married. You weren't even born yet."

Day One, we've completed one of the five boxes needing acknowledgment.

We adjourn. I have to re-organize the boxes, in accordance with the lists, to make the coin exchange go faster. It takes about seventeen hours for me to do that. We come back the next week.

As each page is completed, Mr. Bohdan Buriak signs, witnesses sign. Toward the end of the second day, he begins to deflate. It is almost as if the anger is going out of the balloon. This was the last thing he has to hold onto, his anger over the coins. He begins to understand that the marriage is at an end. He finally realizes that once these coins are done, it is done. *We are done.* This will be the last time we sit in the same room together. I am not going to search him out. He is never going to search me out. There is never going to be any hide-and-seek, seek-and-find. We have no reason to see each other, ever again. No action. No reaction. We are done. Stopped. Ended. Too tired even to feel sad.

The Ultimate Revenge

I forgive him. Something Bohdan will never do.

I feel really sorry for him. He's going to end up a miserable old man.

Oh well, that's his funeral.

Because he doesn't have any outside interests. All Bohdan can do is sit and stew. I'm too bloody busy. I have my Ukrainian dancing. My needlepoint. My Ukrainian singing. My Ukrainian women's organization, which is like a sisterhood.

I forgive him. He will never reciprocate.

He would first have to forgive himself, as I have forgiven myself. Have come to be at peace with myself. And so:

Peace be with you, Bohdan.

Dead silence.

Peace be with you, Bohdan.

Dead silence.

Peace be with you, Bohdan.
A monument to cold storage silence.

Katie Zdybel

THE CRITICS

When they were kids, Audrey and Skyla liked to put on shows. Skyla had a super-symmetrical Shirley Temple face, with metallic green eyes and a button-mushroom nose. She'd been the kind of child who delighted adults with her willingness to perform. "A doll," Audrey's mother, Barb, often called her. You could ask Skyla to sing a song from the choir, and she would, adding jazz hands or a cocked hip for flair.

The shows consisted of corralling their parents into dining room chairs while the girls dressed up and fluttered around, playing background music on the stereo, talking up a performance which they had scantly planned. Often there were capes, batons, glitter, and lipstick. At some point, they sang.

When Skyla was in front of their parents performing, Audrey stood behind her, mouthing the words, her arms glued to her sides. She saw the look on her mother's face, total rapture when she watched Skyla, and a coaxing, pleading look for Audrey. "What a card!" Barb would say, later on, when Skyla's teenage quips and snarks were just the right combination of sugar and salt.

Skyla's mother, Lesley, usually didn't make it through the shows. She'd sit frowning, as though trying to sort out how she'd ended up there, then excuse herself, saying she had to get some work done. That's when Skyla would bring out the big guns: a cartwheel that ended in somewhat painful-looking splits.

Later, as teenagers, the two girls' families went on trips together from Halifax to Boston or Toronto, and their parents let the girls go off on their own for an afternoon. Audrey's mother, who fretted over her children, seemed to think Audrey was safe as long as she was with Skyla, while Skyla's mother expected smart behaviour at all times and assumed Audrey would keep Skyla in line. The girls failed on both accounts: within moments Audrey would become flustered and disoriented. Skyla had a way of leading her around, making jokes about the scariness of subways, lingering around the doorways to bars, or even strip clubs, just to make a nervous Audrey laugh.

That was when they invented the Game: following people around, criticizing or adoring their clothing, guessing at their lives, daring each other to talk to a stranger. Audrey never did, but Skyla would saunter up to anyone, and she once took a cigarette out of a man's mouth, putting it in her own.

"How do you do that?" Audrey asked her.

"Easy." Skyla shrugged. "It's just a game."

Skyla and Audrey lived together their last year of university at Dalhousie. They had a roommate, Kaitlyn, who announced at the end of spring semester that in a few weeks she was taking a train from the east coast to the west. Audrey glanced up from her cornflakes and coffee. "The West Coast?"

Neither Audrey nor Skyla had made post-graduation plans – the general pattern was that once Skyla had made a major life decision, Audrey's would follow. But Skyla had been avoiding the topic and seemed reluctant even to say which of her electives – English, theatre, psychology – most interested her.

The words "Vancouver" and "train" struck a bell in Audrey's head and she found herself imagining sitting at a train window with a hardcover novel in her lap, curving through the landscape into a mist of mammoth trees.

Skyla, with her sharp green irises, scanned Audrey's face.

"You don't have the balls," Skyla said, and Audrey blinked.

"For what?"

"I know what you're thinking. There's no way you could do something like that." Skyla smiled brightly at Kaitlyn. "But how fun for you, Kaitlyn."

Audrey stirred cream into her coffee. Across the table, Kaitlyn buttered her toast. When Skyla dumped her dishes in the sink with a clatter and left, shouting over her shoulder that she'd be sleeping at her parents', Kaitlyn said: "Watch out for her. She's got it in for you."

Audrey startled: "She's just...like that sometimes. Skyla and I have been friends since we were three. We're practically family."

"So what?"

Audrey sipped her coffee and looked the other way, her chin slightly lifted, slowly, as though she'd been asked a question too absurd to answer. She'd seen Grace Kelly make this move in a film when someone's remark threw her for a loop. *So what, indeed*, she was thinking. Was it possible being best friends at three and 13 didn't add up to being friends at 23? Why hadn't she thought to ask herself this before?

A few days later, Audrey announced she was joining Kaitlyn on the train. She got dizzy thinking about it. *Go west for the summer*. And do what? She wasn't sure. And be there all alone? *Yes!* She kept sipping sparkling water to settle her stomach, but now that she'd said it, she couldn't retract it. And didn't want to. The idea was like a cultured pearl in the palm of her hand that she was slowly closing her fingers around.

In Audrey's bedroom in the apartment they shared, Skyla sat on the bed, crunching carrot sticks, watching Audrey pack.

"I was thinking I might move to Toronto in the fall." *Crunch.* "I'm just saying, don't count on me being here when you get back. I was thinking of just going for the summer, but what's the point? A summer's nothing."

Audrey smoothed out a cardigan, folding it in a neat square before placing it in her suitcase. She did a mental check: clothes for warm weather, rain, job interviews, spontaneous dates. "Aren't you applying to med school?"

Skyla flung herself backward on the bed dramatically, growling, "I'm sick of talking about med school!"

Audrey rolled a braided leather belt into a tight coil. "Your mom's just trying to help. She doesn't think you're motivated about pursuing anything else—"

Skyla barked out a laugh. "Thanks for telling me what my own mom thinks about me."

"Well," Audrey pressed her lips together and looked around the room. "What is it that you want to do?" It felt risky to ask this of Skyla. She'd never said what she wanted to be and there was a hard shell around the topic as though it was something too delicate to speak of. There had been a time when Skyla confided in her, but that was beginning to seem like a long time ago.

Skyla touched at a large pimple on her chin, absently, and then turned to bury her face in a pillow. Just as quickly, she shot up, grabbed another carrot stick, and pretended to smoke it like a cigarette – not in a juvenile way, but in a convincing, cinematic way – while peering into Audrey's suitcase. "God, you pack like my grandmother. Making sure you have an outfit for every occasion." She blew imaginary smoke from the corner of her lips. "What's this one for?" She pulled out a pencil skirt and crisp blouse from the bottom of the stack, upsetting everything parcelled out on top of it.

Audrey pressed her lips. "Museums."

Skyla threw her head back, laughing. Carrot flew from her mouth. "Well, don't forget your pearls! Seriously, Kaitlyn's old aunt will be thrilled to have a new best friend."

Audrey flicked the bit of carrot from the top of her travel jewellery case. "I'm not staying with Kaitlyn and her aunt in Vancouver. I'm going on my own to Victoria."

In a high school textbook there had been pictures of the old Victoria hotel, The Empress; she'd wanted to go to Victoria ever since. It seemed like a place with an aesthetic that was polished and regal. She imagined meeting someone in the lobby – the carpet would be plush underfoot. She'd wear an A-line skirt and kitten heels – with no Skyla there to make fun of her preference for classic fashion.

She was aware of Skyla gawping at her, and felt a ripple of satisfaction.

But then Skyla hauled herself up off the bed and stood so close to Audrey their toes touched. "You won't last two weeks on your own. You're too afraid of everything."

She wanted to say, "I'm not, anymore," but it wasn't quite true and her throat suddenly felt thick. She stood looking at Skyla's face, so intimately familiar to her, and thinking how, up this close, all she could see were the blemishes.

Audrey's dad and Skyla's mother were doctors at the hospital. That was how the two families first met. Skyla had grown up in a turreted Victorian near Point Pleasant Park, the expensive end of Halifax. To get into their yard, Audrey had to punch a code into a wrought-iron gate. Skyla's mother, Lesley, wore high heels that tick-tocked on the shiny floors. Audrey marvelled at her hair – a bold, premature white, cut with razor-precision in an angle across her forehead. She was not exactly warm.

Audrey's mother, Barb, on the other hand, had shoulder-length, butterscotch hair that she wore in a butterfly clip, half up, half down. She was usually in slippers and hand-knit sweaters. Seemingly content, she had been a stay-at-home mom, taking care of Audrey and her five brothers and sisters with craft projects, park outings, and baking. The house was full of rockets made from paper towel rolls, paper plates stuck with glitter and spiral pasta, now many years old. Skateboards, hockey sticks, paperbacks, clarinet and violin cases had settled on top of the first layer of debris. Barb kept it all. She loved scrapbooking; she cried when one Mother's Day she discovered the family had secretly converted a walk-in closet into "Scrapbook Headquarters" (this is what the sign on the door read). More often than not, Barb forgot to ask Audrey how school was going and when Audrey told her she wanted to do her master's, her mother seemed a bit perplexed.

"For what?"

Audrey, home for dinner, was sitting at the kitchen table with her mother, father, and the three brothers who were still in high school She was leaving in the morning for Victoria on the train.

"English."

"No," Barb said, "I mean, what do you need a master's for?

"Well, it would help me get a better job for one thing. But for another, I want to keep studying literature."

Barb, salad bowl in hand, seemed to be mulling over Audrey's words.

"Well, I think it is a fine idea," Audrey's dad said. "You should check out the universities in Victoria and Vancouver this summer."

"You wouldn't move all the way out there, though, dear. Would you, Audrey? I thought this was just a little trip. For the summer? You can do a master's here – can't you?"

Audrey leaned back and crossed her legs. "I might move out there," she said, a trill of nervousness running through her.

"But there's no family out there," Barb protested. "Where will you go for Thanksgiving dinner?"

Audrey looked at her mother, floral oven mitts on both hands and an apron that said WILL COOK FOR KISSES. Home-cooked meals, family gatherings, recipes, household chores, and the occasional stolen moment to watch *The View* or read her *Shopaholic* books – Audrey saw her mother's day clearly. If they'd been playing their game, Audrey thought, Skyla would have said: "Housewife," in a tone that meant that *housewife* is not a thing to be proud of. Or perhaps, Audrey realized with discomfort, that was how she saw her own mother. Skyla had never criticized Barb; if and when Audrey complained about her mother, Skyla just listened.

Then Audrey thought of Lesley, Skyla's mother: assertive, imperious, sharp. What would Skyla have called her? "CEO," Audrey would have said, meaning *powerful*. What Skyla would say came to Audrey a moment later: ice queen or, possibly, bitch.

Her mother was still staring at her, mouth hanging open in a way that annoyed Audrey. "Honey? Why would you move all the way out there?"

"To. Study. Literature," Audrey said, as though she were talking to a child. Her dad shot her a sharp look and she dropped her eyes to her plate, knowing she should feel guilty.

Audrey hadn't grown into her length until they'd started university, about the same time she'd stopped hiding behind her bangs. Her figure became less stick-like and more lithe, making everything she wore look interesting, distinctive. She developed a look for reserved, well-tailored clothes – a look she admired in old film noir movies – and soon other girls tried mimicking her style.

Skyla, on the other hand, had puffed out after she started university. And then, quite suddenly, Skyla's face bloomed with acne – the angry-looking kind. It started as a trail of pus-filled whiteheads along her chin and then spread all over her face, exploding into oily red mounds, leaving pockmarks where she picked at them. When she tried to cover them up, it looked like she'd spackled beige cottage cheese onto her cheeks.

Lesley was a dermatologist, but she hadn't taken much interest in Skyla's battle with her face. "Smarten up," is what Lesley said to Skyla's young adult sass. Her skin got worse and worse.

Around the time they graduated from Dalhousie, it was Barb – noticing how the acne crippled Skyla's confidence – who bought Skyla a skincare kit she'd seen advertised on TV. The box promised a clear, radiant complexion.

Skyla looked at the kit. "Results in six months," she read flatly.

Barb put her arm around Skyla's hunched shoulders. "I know it seems like a long time, dear, but—"

Skyla looked up. "Six months," she said again, her whole face changing, illuminating. "I can do six months." She leaned into Barb's arm.

Around the same time, as Audrey learned to roll her shoulders back and lift her chin, Lesley began to take notice of her. A few weeks before leaving for Victoria, Audrey dropped by the big house to visit Skyla. Lesley was at the dining-room table where she often worked. She leaned back in her chair, and Audrey could feel her watching as she crossed the foyer. Lesley called: "Audrey. "

Audrey was wearing a black turtleneck, slim on her slender figure, and black pants cropped above her small, smooth ankle bones, black ballet flats. It was an Audrey Hepburn day. Lesley studied her a moment, her glasses off, but held between one finger and thumb. "Have you given any consideration to law or political science. Journalism?"

Audrey rolled the question around in her mind, pleasantly. "I like reading best. I've tried to write my own stories, but it doesn't come naturally."

"What do you like about reading exactly?"

Again, the question was like a treat. She savoured it before responding, "I like picking a story apart. Deciding for myself whether it's...effective or not." She was pleased at choosing a more erudite word than *good.*

Lesley nodded, the architectural bangs grazing one high cheekbone. "What do you consider effective in contemporary American literature?" And so on, until Audrey had been sitting there for 45 minutes, dissecting Roxane Gay, Lauren Groff, Rebecca Solnit. Skyla, coming downstairs to find Audrey with her mom, was agitated.

"What the hell were you two talking about?" she asked as Audrey followed her back upstairs.

"Female voices in American literature and their effect on—"

Skyla halted. "No school talk outside of school, remember?"

On her last night in Halifax, Audrey went to a friend's house for a party. It was a going-away party for Audrey and Kaitlyn.

Josh was there – he and Skyla had dated earlier in the year, Audrey having a crush on him all the while. But after things cooled between Josh and Skyla, Audrey never quite got up the courage to ask him out. Or rather, she'd never had the nerve to ask Skyla if it was okay to ask him out.

Skyla got drunk in a drinking game. Audrey took little sips of her wine cooler and Skyla snorted.

"Look at Little Miss Priss over there." She took a swig of beer with her pinky finger sticking out. "Oh, I would never get smashed!" she exclaimed in dramatic modesty, in a British accent for flair. A few people laughed in a sort of uncommitted way, but Josh frowned and set his unfinished drink down on the table and went into the kitchen. "Come dance with me, Audrey!" he called over his shoulder.

Audrey had a look of surprise – Skyla went on with the act, changing her accent to Southern belle: "Who? Li'l ol' me?" she asked, fluttering her eyelashes and pressing her fingers to her chest. But she elbowed someone's beer bottle while doing it and drew back from the splash. "Fuck! I'm all gross now! Thanks a lot, Audrey." She got up without wiping the beer or apologizing and everyone around the table looked at each other awkwardly before wandering into the kitchen.

Josh was dancing the way a funny uncle or kindergarten teacher might, not trying to look cool, just wanting to make Audrey laugh, and it was working. As she slid from her perch on the counter to join him, Skyla came grinding up behind Josh, pushing her hips into his ass, but still making a puckered-lip ingenue face, holding her pinky out. "Oh my! Look at me, everyone! I'm touching a man's bum!" She cracked into sharp laughter, looking around for someone to join her.

Someone turned the music up and then they couldn't hear her.

A little later, they walked home, Skyla lurching in clunky high heels. "Imagine how huge a zit would look on the big screen," she slurred, leaning into Audrey and then laughing as though she'd made a joke. Her eyes searched Audrey's.

"What?" Audrey asked, reaching out to steady her.

"The film of the year," Skyla said in movie voice-over, "starring… Skyla Roberts's acne." She snickered and tottered.

Audrey looked at her friend and for the first time saw what the acne was doing to her. "Skyla—"

"Remember the Game, Audrey?" Skyla asked suddenly. "What would we say about me now?" She laughed sharply and then said nothing the rest of the way.

The next morning Audrey tapped on Skyla's door, lightly, but heard no answer, just the phlegmy sound of hangover snoring.

Somewhere in Manitoba, on the train west, Kaitlyn brought it up. They were sharing a pot of tea and a bag of M&Ms. Or rather, Kaitlyn was munching on the candy; Audrey picked the occasional one out of the bag and sucked on it. Kaitlyn said, "Skyla told me you said I was getting fat."

"You are not fat, Kaitlyn."

Kaitlyn shrugged. "But did you say it?"

Audrey paused, her teacup partway to her mouth. "*No*," she said. "Of course not."

"So then why'd Skyla say you did?"

"She really said that?"

"Yeah. And you know what else? Skyla told Emily that you said she wore cheap, shitty clothes and looked like a homeless person."

Audrey glared. "What? When?"

"And she told Ivy that you said the hair on her head looks like pubic hair."

Audrey almost laughed except she could see how serious Kaitlyn was. "When did all this happen?"

"Recently. I told you...she has it in for you." There was a glint in Kaitlyn's eye that caught Audrey's attention. She wasn't making it up, Audrey thought, but she was enjoying delivering the news.

"I would never say those things."

It hadn't started that way, but the Game had become cruel. When they had played, sitting in a pub in Halifax, or attending a big event on campus, Skyla would say: "That guy, he's a tech freak. Lives in a basement and masturbates all day. And she's a 40-year-old single woman who can't get a date; she watches *Legends of the Fall* while eating raw cookie dough, like twice a week."

Skyla's crassness unnerved Audrey, but at the same time, it felt like a challenge. She tried her hand at it: "He wears mom jeans. She paid twenty bucks for her haircut." But Skyla would snicker at her and call her a prude. Audrey had no gift for zingers – she couldn't say words like "masturbate" or "porn," not as naturally as Skyla – but she was good at critiquing. She studied people and often wished she could give them advice: cover your roots; don't wear Gore-Tex when you're not camping; learn how to hold a fork; try not to use slang, and never ever pass gas in front of others.

But she never said things like that about people they knew. Only strangers. Skyla had told Audrey that Emily was a bad dresser and Audrey had thought to herself, *She looks cheap*. And with Ivy, too, Skyla had laughed when their friend had walked away and whispered to Audrey, "That haircut looks hideous on her." And Audrey had thought, just *thought*, to herself: *Her hair is too dark and wiry for that cut.*

If Skyla knew she thought those things, did she also know what Audrey was thinking about her, now? That she was glad Skyla had gotten acne – the blow that rearranged their pecking order – and that she was glad Skyla never had her kind of conversations with Lesley.

Audrey had arranged a house-sit and part-time job in Victoria through a family connection. She spent her first evening organizing the house, putting things into cupboards in tidy lines and stacks. She could hear Skyla in her ear: "Oh, lighten up, Audrey. You're so anal." Audrey hated the word. "Bum" she could take, but "anal" made her think of colonoscopies and hemorrhoid cream.

Her job at the bookstore started three days after she arrived in Victoria. She could have taken the bus, but she preferred to walk. The differentness of the West was a revelation to her. The air felt clean and mossy in her nose, her skin became dewy and her hair puffed up, but she tamed it, shiny and straight, into a glossy ponytail.

On her walk that morning, Audrey felt a pang for Skyla – the old Skyla. They would have followed the woman in front of them in her high-heeled boots, a leather clutch under her arm, a trench coat cinched tightly around a thin figure, wondering what her story was.

"Fashion designer," Audrey would have said.

"Stockbroker by day, stripper by night."

Or Skyla might have said something more cutting, and Audrey would have had to sort out that uncomfortable feeling that lay somewhere between disapproval and thrilling agreement.

She said to Josh on the phone one evening, "I just wanted to make sure you knew I didn't say those things."

"Everybody who knows you, knows those are Skyla's words, not yours. You're the nice one, Audrey. Have you talked to her?"

"No."

"Well, good. You know, I love the old Skyla, but this new one's a bully. She's just jealous of you and making you pay for it."

Audrey blanched, a sudden fizz in her stomach. "She couldn't be jealous of me." But she realized as she said it that she was trying to draw him out, and Josh walked right into it, assuring her for the next few minutes that she had bypassed Skyla in likeability and coolness.

"Would you even be friends with her if your families weren't so close?" he asked.

She swallowed, unsure how best to respond.

"I mean, I get that you two have history," he said, "but if you met her today for the first time, honestly, what would you think of her?"

She selected the words carefully, knowing Josh didn't go for mean, and yet, here was the chance to throw the stone to sink the ship. "I think I'd feel sorry for her."

Josh was quiet for a moment and she felt her stomach twist – perhaps she'd laid it on too thick. But then he said, "See? Even when you have a right to be angry, you're still nice."

It is *easy*, she thought.

By the time she hung up the phone, her stomach hurt and her teeth ached, like she'd indulged in too much candy.

The bookstore where she worked part-time was busy. The manager, Lee, a quirky but focused businesswoman and bibliophile, took a liking to Audrey. She noticed when Audrey reorganized a section so that it displayed better or knew exactly what book to recommend to a customer. She agreed to write a reference letter for Audrey's University of Victoria grad studies application, and in it had called Audrey *eloquent, discerning,* and *refined.* Lovely words. She kept rolling them through her mind like ticker tape.

"You've got great taste," she said to Audrey one grey August day, when Audrey had been there three months. Audrey was structuring a display of Young Adult reads, bypassing the popular vampire-witch-and-wizard fare for classics.

"Lee, I saw a photograph at Delia's place where I'm house-sitting. It showed her in front of a big sign that said CLARION BOOKS. Is that another bookstore in town?"

"That was the name of her company," Lee said. "Delia was a critic. She reviewed books for the provincial papers."

Audrey froze, her arms full of books. It was like a gear suddenly clicked into place in her brain. *That's me!* She couldn't believe she had never thought of herself as a critic before.

She realized later, when she scurried outside on her morning break to call Skyla's house on her cell phone, that if she had really wanted to tell Skyla, she would have called the apartment. But she didn't. She called Skyla's house and she felt her heart trip when it was Skyla who picked up.

"Hey," Skyla said flatly.

Audrey opened her mouth, but then pressed it closed again.

"What's up, Audrey?"

She knew Skyla would belittle her discovery; she'd have some small piece of convincing evidence to prove Audrey would never be a good book critic.

"If you're calling to tell me you talked to Emily and Ivy and Josh, I already know." There was a snorting sound. "You'll be glad to know none of them are speaking to me. The summer's been a blast."

On the street, people swished past her.

"Calling me up to chew me out and you can't say a word, can you? Well, guess what, Audrey? I didn't say anything to anybody that you wouldn't have said yourself—"

Audrey shook her head. "I wouldn't say those things." Her voice broke, but she kept going. "I didn't say those things. That's the difference between you and me."

Skyla, quiet as a whisper, said, "And you think that makes you better than me, don't you? I'm so crude and you're so nice and demure and everybody just loves you. Is that what you think? Well, guess what? Thinking what you thought makes you just as crude as me."

Audrey leaned over, there on the sidewalk, one arm wrapped around her waist.

Skyla went on: "I know what you think of me and I know what you think of all our friends. I know what you think of your own mother: You're embarrassed by her." It sounded like Skyla was crying, something Audrey hadn't heard for years. There was a moan and then a pause and then the voice went hard again. "Maybe no one else knows how you think, but I do, so just remember that, Miss Perfect, Miss Refined. I know what you're thinking and you're a foul-mouthed little—"

Audrey hung up. Her hand shook and she felt an incredible heat in her throat; her head buzzed. She couldn't hold it in, and if she tried, she felt like she'd burn from the inside out. She held out the phone and yelled at it, there on the street: "You're a fucking cunt, Skyla Roberts!" She stopped, suddenly aware that bookstore customers walking past had paused. Her voice had been shrill, screeching up and away from her. Lee was at the doorway, staring at her, looking as though she'd tasted something rancid.

Audrey put her hand to her throat. A wash of feelings went through her: She felt ill, but also somehow lighter. Embarrassed, but then – no. Something hardened around that feeling. She flashed, of all things, to Skyla's child-self, swinging her arms wildly while lip-syncing to Madonna, nudging Audrey and giving her that wink, like *You can do this, Audrey. Just watch me.* Barb, leaning forward in her seat, expectant, hopeful.

She smoothed a palm along her pulled-back hair, then walked up the steps past Lee, her back straight. "I'm sorry about that. I had a personal matter to attend to."

Lee hesitated a moment, then gave a slow nod. "In the future—" she began, but Audrey cut her off crisply, even severely:

"*Of course.*"

For about a year after the summer she moved to Victoria, Audrey tried to get in touch with Lesley without going through Skyla, but she never got any emails or phone calls back. Eventually, Audrey decided Lesley was being loyal to Skyla. Or maybe it was what happened when you moved to the other end of the country. She had lost touch with the others, too, even Josh.

It felt increasingly rude of her mother to bring Skyla up on the phone. "Skyla was by today. She got the part she auditioned for. We're so thrilled! We're taking her to lunch to celebrate tomorrow."

"We?"

"Lesley will come, too. She loved Skyla in that last play. She especially loved the rave reviews!"

Audrey was sitting in her cubicle, a pile of papers in front of her criss-crossed with red-penned comments. "Mother, I really don't have time to chit-chat now," she said. For a moment, she stared at the plastic partitions around her and thought about how silly it was, that if she wanted to she could just kick one over. How flimsy and insubstantial.

"All right, well, don't work too hard, Audrey. Get out and make some friends!"

She caught her reflection in the window across from her desk. *What would we say about me now? Overly ambitious? Bitch? Alone.* She tugged at her fitted jacket and ran her pointing finger over an eyebrow, pressed her red lips together too hard. "What excellent advice, Mother." The last word wobbled.

Her mother was quiet for a moment on the other end, then: "Oh, Audrey, dear…"

Audrey shook her head curtly and hung up the phone.

But that wasn't the worst of it. It was what they both, as girls, would have said about Skyla – *the* Skyla Roberts, up-and-comer. What the reviews said. Audrey had read them, too, of course. She had even clipped one out: *Radiant! Outshines all others. May as well have been the only one on the stage.* Every time she read it, in her mind, the voice was her mother's.

Marion Quednau

SUNDAY DRIVE TO GUN CLUB ROAD

At one time, when owning a car was still a big deal, and gas cheap, land even cheaper – you could buy acres of the stuff, with scrub trees and a gouged-out gravel pit, for a song – taking a drive was the classic pastime. Or so my father once told me. On Saturday, he said, it was the kids' job to wash the car for the big outing, flinging soap at one another, earning their paltry allowances. Sunday you got behind the wheel after filing out of church, pressed by something you couldn't name, as though you had to make a run for it, get somewhere and fast. If you took to the back roads, all that blather about salvation that had hurt your ears while the smarmy pastor droned on and on would just fly out the windows, my father said. He liked to joke about things.

Long after churchgoing had fizzled – the white clapboard husk of St. Mary's on our street stood mainly hollow and empty, only a few blue-hairs straggling in to pray for people like ourselves, spiritually lost – my family still had the habit of hitting the road. It was nearly the end of a century famous for gas-guzzling and wasting time between wars, but we had a pent-up energy on Sundays to get going, be somewhere.

I thought of our aimless trips along the shimmering roads as one of those wavy pencil illusions when you waggle your fingers just to impress yourself because nobody else cares. Or like some head-hurting math problem: how long will it take this family to reach any sort of destination, given a few random detours, like us nearly hitting a bear cub once, my mother shrieking, "Oh, for the love of Martha!" and the grim fact that the car burned oil, constantly needed topping up. Our being together in a moving vehicle was an act of faith, one my father believed would assign us a history, save us from being unremarkable as a family. We'd go zooming down some potholed country road, in any old direction in any blunted weather, and simply stare out the windows of our old clunker Oldsmobile as if we were watching our favourite TV show, *The Passing Scenery*.

After a few hours of looking for God knows what, we'd stop somewhere, maybe at an old diner called The Hilltop or The Rendezvous, one of those places still serving real pies or big milkshakes from a noisy retro blender on the counter. And for a while that became the gambit, where we could find such a homey place, with pan-fries and my father's old faves – creamed chicken on toast or fried liver with onions. Once, we drove south of the line to some hole-in-the-wall near Snohomish, Washington, but a cop pulled us over for "rubbernecking," as he called it. Asked us what "our business" was, the state trooper not nearly as friendly as our Canadian Mountie sort. He didn't laugh when my father said, "What, do we look like potheads?" So we stayed north of the border, looking for sudden roadside rewards, what we seemingly deserved.

It couldn't be fast food – my father had no patience for the overly sweet slop that all tasted the same. "You call this pathetic little morsel a burger?" he'd said once, the girl behind the take-out window sliding it shut on his fingers. It was part of my father's shtick to be a food critic, an everything critic. I had this odd feeling he wasn't just trying to entertain us, but show us something that needed watching.

I noticed he never complained about my mother's cooking; she always packed a few things with a chunk of dry ice in the cooler: sandwiches with fatty deli meats, her gloppy potato salad, a few pieces of nearly spoiled fruit. In good weather, we'd find a picnic spot and chow down, kick a ball about for a bit, listen to the birds or watch someone chasing a headlong dog, trying to call it back.

I don't remember how the house thing started. More than once my father rolled down the window, took a deep breath, and spoke of getting a farm, growing our own food, that whole back-to-the-land thing where enterprising sorts could be smarter than the average joe, self-sufficient. He taunted my mother with leaving his job, but after the look of alarm on her face he left that topic alone. He'd worked for the railroad since forever, new technologies and old decrepit trains making his stints as signal man or conductor, yard master or bridge inspector, ever more erratic; he'd been transferred more than promoted, that's how my mother put it. Still, he stood to get a decent pension for all the runaround. So maybe they were both thinking of the future, how it could look different when we went toodling along some gravel road north of nowhere.

I know the first time we wandered into one of those public showings of houses that needed selling – and fast – we were hooked. By the risky notion, perhaps, of people's hopes so exposed. As if someone might buy six rooms and a specialty koi pond or flagstoned breezeway on impulse. Or maybe with a vengeance, like a drive-by shooting. Something simmering in the back of their minds they've meant to do for a long time.

We'd scoff and roll our eyes at the so-called "staging" of rooms, everything that might describe the average tacky family tucked away in cupboards while flowers swayed in vases, a kitschy plaque displayed over the scorched fireplace that stopped burning wood eons ago, saying IMAGINE! or THERE'S NO PLACE LIKE HOME.

"Those signs are majorly annoying," my sister Amy piped up after we'd had our fill of crescent-shaped moons in bedrooms promising SWEET DREAMS or paddle-shaped folk art saying BEACH when you were nowhere near water, or even worse when you were – the house on a jutting cliff with no way down to the Pacific rolling in below. "Sweatshop-made by kids barely old enough to go to school in some nasty burb of Bangkok or Shanghai. And they *don't* – go to school, I mean. They just make shit like that for rich people to close deals on houses. It makes me sick."

She was going through her idealistic, clean-up-her-act phase. But my mother told her she shouldn't swear in front of my younger brother, a gnarly 11-year-old stuck between his sisters in the back seat, reading crime comics and laughing giddily at some murder gone wrong.

To my mind, the near-empty, freshly scented rooms with lavender-painted walls without scuff marks or cobwebs in the corners looked hokey, sure, and you'd hit your shins on the glass coffee tables if you actually lived there. But the fake-fancy stuff wasn't nearly as depressing as the cluttered houses, tons of grandchildren photos and knitted dealies over every chair, obviously the hangout of old folks about to move into rest homes. Or maybe even keeled over, suddenly dead and gone. It made me sad to think the knick-knacks might be all that remained of their lives, ceramic cock-a-doodle doodads for holding spoons, amber glass ashtrays from when it was still cool to smoke indoors and give your newborn a stroke from all the fumes.

My sister Amy was good to have along on these outings, because she was more and more obviously "expecting." Her soccer-ball tummy with its pierced belly button poking out of her shorty T-shirts made people think we were serious, maybe even desperate, about this house-buying business. Not just kicking tires.

My dad laughingly called her condition "knocked up," despite my mother frowning and saying it wasn't polite – or even respectful to Amy. She said it as though good manners and leaving someone to make their own mistakes were two different notions.

"It used to mean, 'woken up,' someone banging on the shutters to get you out of bed, back in Shakespeare's day," my father replied. "And in that sense, I would say Amy is well and truly 'knocked up.'"

He chortled again, because he always found himself amusing. And expected us to be onside, or else he got hurt feelings, just like a big kid. So my mother's tight laugh, just to keep him company, often started ahead of the punchline. She was an appeaser, if not an outright enabler. Hitler might have been worse if she'd been his mother.

"Who'd live on Gun Club Road?" my father protested after we'd traipsed around a living room with lumpy wall-to-wall carpet, browning at the edges, and bedrooms with no sheets on the beds. Just bare mattresses, as if the name of the road had made someone move out in a big hurry. Monster truck repossessed, and the deadbeat renters walking a fine line between petty thieving and real crime.

"Yes, that one's definitely out," my mother agreed, as if actually discussing the pros and cons of the neighbourhood.

There was another open house just one street over, on Marble Road.

"I have a hunch that old crook of a realtor is a hard-core closer on deals with leaking basements and parasites under the laminate flooring," my dad said, when we left the place with complacent smiles and headed to our ages-old dinosaur of a car. I mean, the car alone should have given us away.

"Too Italian," my mother said of the kitchen, "and I don't get the big shift toward granite counters. They stain like crazy, red wine, fruit juices, you name it. Besides, I don't like my kitchen to be too show-offy."

"Yeah, the place was a little over-the-top," I agreed. "As if a cheap rancher can look like a villa near Rome. More like the fall of Rome! Ha-ha!" I was starting to sound like my joke-a-minute father. Trying too hard.

There was a front seat discussion then about where the best granite came from – whether from eastern Canada, in Quebec my mother thought, or some quarry in India or Brazil my father countered, where they don't have to deal with the environmental rigmarole. "The poor sods mining the stuff die of lung diseases from all the dust," my father added, as if he were suddenly the greenest guy on earth.

"Who was it that said luxury should feel like comfort?" my mother asked, waggling her head around in small circles, as though her neck might be kinked by all of our far-fetched travels.

"Coco Chanel," my sister offered. "And it must have been an afterthought, 'cause she had a shitty life, despite all the parties on the Riviera and the glitzy jewels. Never found her happy place."

It was something Amy had read in her fashion mags, no doubt.

I could see my mother want to curb Amy's blunt language again, but she changed the shape of her mouth and her mind along with it, suddenly admitted she was uncomfortable with *this whole thing*.

"What whole thing?" my father asked.

"Taking our shoes off and tiptoeing around people's private spaces. As if we were looking in on their lives and finding them lacking. Judging books by their covers, so to speak."

My mother was master of the blurt, saying something offhand that was really a warning in disguise. It was the only way she could get anyone's attention. As if she'd said something important by accident, and never mind her.

"What – you think we should leave our shoes on?" my father said, trying for a laugh.

"No," my mother said. That was all. Although there was a sparking in the air, like when you forget to rip off the foil from the instant dinner in the microwave.

"Well, the notion of an 'open house,'" my father continued, "is clearly an invitation." He could feel the sting of her reproach, no matter how slight. "These wise-ass realtors are daring folks to be enthralled about the rotten wiring in the basement or the way the deck needed replacing years ago. I can't believe some of these places, and the prices they want. The realtor always saying he'll have to check on the actual *bona fide* lot line or that we can add on in the future, when he's just BS'ing us. It takes a certain nerve – so we shouldn't feel bad."

"Far from it," he added, just so we all got the point.

But my mother didn't quit. I had to admire her sudden show of spunk.

"The last realtor was a woman," she said quietly, "who answered your questions quite handily, I thought." My mother was clearly doing some daring of her own.

My father said nothing more, just firmed up something in his jaw and kept his eyes on the road.

I wanted to fix it between them, agree with my mother's old-fashioned common sense, and still run with my father's bluster. I have to admit I liked looking at other people's updated bathrooms with their little baskets of different coloured soap or their so-called "great rooms" with faux-leather couches and rugs sporting the bright colours of a cheap trip to Mexico. The gas fireplaces with the fake logs lighting up at the press of a button, the spacious sofas with oodles of throw cushions at just the right angle, not too heaped in a pile and not too scattered. I felt relieved to see houses that shiny and polished, like a neat ending to a story, not like our house, always under construction with one of my father's notions to expand the front porch from something bigger than a welcome mat or to make the extra room in the basement into a separate suite for Amy's incoming squawker. As far as I knew, my father liked tearing things down, not so much lifting them up again.

Every now and then we would find a few upscale places in our searches, in recently tree-shorn neighbourhoods called Eagle's Watch or Bonnybrook Place, the homes bigger and newer, more costly and out-of-reach. My father was getting ideas on the road, he would say to us. "Of what *not* to do, hardy-har-har. Like those fake mullioned windows, with their chintzy little plastic inserts? Give me a break."

"That's good," my mother said, humouring him again, as though what had briefly reared up between them was settled. It felt endless, relentless, as if we would always pile into the old Cutlass on Sundays and look for a promising aspect to the landscape, a house perched on a knoll as though it belonged, something that would make us stop, take our shoes off, tread lightly in the sacred spaces of other lives. Then turn around and go home to our so-called "character house" of cracked stucco with fake Tudor beams, the furniture all hand-me-down and mismatched, every room crammed with failed intention to sort or paint, to feel less dissatisfied.

On one of our Sunday jaunts, an elderly couple took a particular shine to our whimsical family, where we all played our parts. My brother, when he got tired or hungry, started acting half his age. Six at best, all whiney and crumpled. So at the umpteenth house of that day's touring – "it is a gracious house, with good bones," the realtor insisted – my brother said aloud, in a hectic voice, "Why aren't there ever more people at these things? I don't get it. Why are we the only ones?"

My father took him aside and said just as loudly, in his typical swashbuckling style, "You know, son, at an open house down near Dallas, Texas, way back in 1952, they offered free Dr. Pepper soft drinks and a Cadillac to the lucky buyer of any brand-spanking-new house in the suburbs they were building. And you know how many people showed up? Thirty thousand. Thirty *thousand.* Now *that* was hoopla!"

My brother was looking blank and his stomach was gurgling. The owners of the house – they hadn't vamoosed like you were supposed to – brought out a plate of tired Oreos. I swear there was dust on the cookies. But my brother dove in.

They were a sad-faced look-alike pair, like John and Yoko, as if people found a certain sameness in a face to make them feel more at home with a stranger. Or how people come to look like their droopy-jowled dogs, so maybe this pair had once had a hound or something. All I know is that they *hovered,* that was the only word for it. Seemed to be assessing the possibilities as we moved from room to room in our stockinged feet and poked at window ledges, flipped light switches on and off.

And they told us things, private things not generally admitted to prospective buyers. How a baby had died in the house in the early years. And how the house itself, with its grand old front porch and radiators hissing in every room, had seemed to shore them up, give them the constitution required to carry on. They'd never had another child – had lost their nerve, so to speak. But the creaking staircases and Victorian gables housing the memories of the child had seemed enough to care for, to speak to, to inhabit.

"That's why it's never been on the market, up for grabs. But since my husband's stroke, well, he needs so many visits to the hospital, we've decided to move close by, have an apartment for the time being. I mean, enough time has passed, it feels as though someone else could care for... our Jimmy," the woman said, her sparse hair permed to a frizz that made her seem fraught, still.

The realtor, who'd been pacing in another room, clearly chagrined with the off-the-rails sellers, had finally broken things off with a spiel about new soffits and a dandy energy-saving gas furnace about to be installed.

"Whoa," my dad said when we hit the car. "That was some sales pitch. And it never seemed to occur to them that Amy is – in the family way," he said, gloating at my mother with his eloquent language, "and might not want to hear that sort of thing."

"People in their grief," my mother muttered.

"I would like to know how the dead baby got that way, I mean, dead," my brother the private detective said, now that his blood sugar was restored.

"What, you think arsenic in his mashed peas, or maybe they locked him in a toy box for using bad words until he turned blue in the face?" I asked, trying to pique my brother into acting normal for once.

"They didn't say his age," my mother broke in, tartly. As if we were finally, after all these years, getting on her nerves. "But he was a baby, they said, so too young to speak much at all."

Our surmising of rusted swing sets and choking on food grew boring by the time we reached the next open house with blue balloons swinging merrily from a tree branch, a windswept sign promising "Free coffee!"

"That's made up my mind already," my father said, giving way to his usual mirth. "Yum, yum. Something on the hotplate since early Jurassic times."

The winding pathway to the house had the sweet smell of rotting pine needles and twisted tree roots all set to trip you up.

"This entrance doesn't lend itself to bringing in the groceries," my sister said. She was eerily starting to sound like a mother, all warning and worry.

And then she suddenly doubled up, made an *arggg* sound, as though someone had just stabbed her in the stomach. She straightened up again, her eyes tearing.

"Wow, that was a doozer," she stammered. "A burning flash in baby-town – as if I just swallowed a shot of brandy on the tip of a knife."

Amy had some potential as a writer, I thought just then. It would be something to kill time while she breastfed. And breastfed.

My father took her by the elbow. As though he would gladly walk her down the aisle if only he could find any reputable young man my sister had never yet met.

I had to wonder how many shots of brandy my sister, at sweet seventeen, had swallowed. And with whom? The mystery father? She'd never said who it was, just burst into tears of rage – it looked like to me – every time the subject came up. Boys of high school drop-out age didn't usually tipple brandy in snifters. So, someone of my father's ripe old vintage? The thought gave me a coy twisting of innards. As though I could feel the kid inside my sister wiggling, insisting the truth come out in a big, sloppy plop.

The house didn't have an easy flow, my father said, pointing to a long dark corridor branching off to a series of small, shadowy rooms.

The realtor was young, full of ideas. "Yeah, I agree. You could knock down a few walls and really open up the space." He smelled of nervous sweat, spruced up with cologne, and my sister started to look a little green in the face.

"We're going outside for a spell," my mother said. "Fresh air."

I could see them through what the realtor called the "retro picture-window" in the low-ceilinged living room. And the picture wasn't pretty. My sister was throwing up in the rock garden, splashing the plants with her plumes of roadside picnic lunch. Always too much salt and mayo, you could count on it with my mother, no matter what the menu.

As distraction, my father led the young fellow toward the kitchen, which smelled of mould and fake-lemon cleaning agents. "So, what about drainage?" he asked, looking up the sloping backyard to the neighbour's back fence looming above, as though the house being pitched as a mid-century, cute-as-a-bug rancher might lie in a gulch or river bottom.

I gave my dad the high sign when my sister had disappeared back toward the car, holding tight to my mother's arm.

We went out the back way so the realtor my father later called "a shifty-eyed young grifter" wouldn't see my sister's display over the hydrangeas. Or smell it.

"Ah, a carport," my father said. "A notion from gentler times."

I knew what he meant, although the realtor looked stymied. I'd once asked my father why garages were the first thing you saw with so many newer houses. And he'd scoffed, as if he couldn't believe the way the world was heading, and said "security," so people could go straight from their locked cars into their locked houses, no fuss, no muss with someone skulking around. I realized I'd been at risk my whole life, getting off my bike in plain view and entering the house by the side door.

"Well, thanks so much," my father said, shaking the realtor's sweaty hand. "Sorry we don't have time for the coffee. We're late for a showing."

"Oh, oh... here's my card," the jumpy guy offered. "Barry – if you have any questions."

My father put the car into high gear, spurting gravel as we departed.

"Feeling any better?" he asked into the rear-view mirror.

"Not much," my sister murmured. Her face was a ghastly grey, with none of that peachy motherly glow.

"I think it's a sign," my mother said, looking directly at my father's right ear.

"That we should skedaddle home? Call it a day?"

"That we should stop doing this – dropping in on a whim. When we have no intention of ever buying any of these... places."

She seemed to be blaming him for something, but I couldn't tell exactly what. A lurid affair came to mind, the kind of secret dalliance that would rear up in the movies and bust a family wide open. But it would have to be a woman as generous as my mother in laughing at bad jokes. And doing it naked, which was highly unlikely.

Everyone in the car went silent, feeling strangely alone in a crowded Oldsmobile smelling ever so faintly of throw-up. Amy was slumping toward the window, her cheek pressed against the glass, the passing scene suddenly struck with bleary spatters of rain.

My brother was cracking his knuckles loudly and making that growly sound in his throat he does when he's trying to stem one of his stupid questions.

"But what would we do – I mean, on Sundays?" He couldn't help himself.

My father sighed a long flubber of an out-breath, sounding like a snorting horse. He seemed to be at a loss for words, which surprised me. He couldn't exactly spell it out, he finally said, how the trips we'd taken were an investment of sorts, in a common vision. But he seemed to be hinting at the fact that we might otherwise be in trouble as a family, might all go our separate ways if not for our playful considerations of this mudroom or that in-law suite. He seemed to be saying that our sightseeing ritual was our church without the church, our roadside redemption.

That was when I noticed the bright stain seeping out from beneath my sister.

"Shit," I croaked out. "Amy's bleeding all over the seat!" Her head was bumping against the glass by now, and she didn't seem to care.

My father did an about-turn and drove like a crazy man toward the hospital only a few minutes to the south. He blared his horn at red lights, green lights and intersections with no lights at all, and gestured with his hands off the wheel at dithering pedestrians, my mother with her head out the window, screaming, "We've got to get to the hospital! Get out of the damn way!"

I'd never heard her swear before, so I knew this was serious.

They took Amy on a stretcher straight from the car, while my clueless brother thought to note aloud that it was just like an *ER* drama on TV, except in real life. My mother gave him a horrified look, as if to say, "Whose child are you?" So he clammed up while my father paced in the waiting room, and my mother tried to look at magazines, but I could see her eyes lifting and peering into the middle distance, measuring something.

Amy pulled through. Of course she did. She's a "tough cookie," as my father would say, which doesn't always sound like a compliment. But the poor little jelly mould of a baby didn't make it. It pissed me off because I'd already spent nights and nights, while falling asleep, trying to name the kid I would probably be babysitting.

And I kept revisiting those houses we'd looked at and talked about. They came back to me, one by one, in that near-dream state when your mind whirls with possibilities. The family room in a big, so-called cottage, with a stone fireplace, the wood stacked neatly beside, ready for flaming. The kitchen nook in another, with its bench seating, like a picnic mood dragged inside. The teensy view of the ocean beyond, its glimmer of light through a dark fringing of woods.

We no longer take Sunday drives, it's true. But we bought a house, a real beaut of an old-timer with hardwood floors and fancy coved ceilings. The one with the dead baby. It has a great backyard with stately old trees where I hang suspended in the saggy old hammock my father strung up. And now, as a family joke, we call Amy's sad day her "Jimmy." Use that day as a marker, to hold our places. Although it's not a name I would have chosen.

Lue Palmer

WATA TIKA DAN BLOOD

"Him come to sin on Sunday. Him wait on Kitty and him wait on Peggy. He talking sound like sweet honey in her ear. And he pretty face look like a sweet sticky trail before he snatch them. Just like that. Wicked!" say the first, Hyacinthe.

"*Eeeee.* Me see done like that before. Is wicked," say the second, Winsome.

Winsome squat up on a rock with her bare leg ankle-deep. Them bare toes pressed under the water that tickle their calf when it splash, wet skirt hoist up in their laps. Them reaching into the water and pulling out of it.

At the soul river, down in the water, where spirit float looking like pools of wet cloth; weaving, bloated and swaying in the water. They floating full like jellyfish around each other. Them colour red. Them colour blue, black, brown, green, purple. They fold in on themself, floating up like they ready for the Judgement Day.

"Well *Iiii* say he not long for the world see. Long since pass we decide what fi do with him now," say the third, Merle. She was not amused; always concern with comings and goings, rights and wrongs.

"No one can say," say Hyacinthe. "Wickedness, it come and it go. No saying when or why."

Them reach into the water, pull out the soul cloths. Them spread the cloths each out and lay them flat. Using them hands to smell the surface. Their wrinkles run across it feeling the fibres hungry, it like the lacing of skin and tissue. They listening, listening for song and greeting. The threads of each cloth chatting out the tune of a lifetime.

Hyacinthe reach into the water and pull out a soul cloth. It small, the thread run short, the weaving cut off before the bottom sew up. She spread it out and look it over, Winsome and Merle leaning to look at the pickney soul, laying with the water soak up. Hyacinthe look at he life, hanging in the short thread. She read he story sad. She breathe heavy and put he back in the water. "We pray next time he fate be kinder," Winsome say. They put he soul cloth in the water, and send he gently down the river bend.

Many them put back in the water, bless them, and push them down the river. But other they ring them quick like a snap neck, like pulling the colour from the cloth deh throat. They feed them to the water, sink them down where the river bed swallow them whole. And the river bottom hungry today.

Some soul them fuss and fight on. "This woman never have a kind word for no one," say Hyacinthe. "The only time she talk to she neighbours when she have gossip!"

"If gossip be a sin then we ought to throw you down the river bottom with her!" say Merle. They fussing and fighting. Winsome snatch the cloth up and push it rough down the river. She grab a stick and jook it round the bend.

Merle sit down pon the rock. She drag up a cloth from the water. It light blue. She sweep it up and naked it come. She look it real close. She poke her tongue out and she taste it. She press it to her face the same way she tilt a cheek to the sweet sun. She hold it close to her chest and rock it from side to side.

Hyacinthe and Winsome crane their necks. "Merle, who that you got there?"

Merle press her lips tight. "Nobody!"

"There's no one so important as a nobody," Hyacinthe call back. Winsome reach over and drag up the blue cloth and lay him out across the stone. The thread criss and cross. Some part shine in the sun, some part rip and ragged. She spread him out end to end, stretched flat and full. And he lay still, quivering in the water cool breeze.

The three look down upon him. Merle hand twist in her lap as they look – her baby boy come to meet he judgement time. "Get on with it," they say. Merle begin slow, reading the soul threads, for the story of her son spread out naked across the rock.

"Huncle he was a sweet boy," she begin. *"He like sorrel juice, and Christmas dinner, cool breeze, and riding he bike in the summertime."* She stop, and Winsome continue.

"An he grew to be a sweetman, dey says. Someone who can hear the coo of a young woman sigh, and know just where to touch her waist, know just how to wring her wrist, and just how to eye her thigh and fatness to make her walk quick – make her head lower and speak hush.

"He knew a lot about cover curtain and roll-down car window and swimming pool corner. He knew what kinda sweet juice look tasty in the summer and how to spend a dime on a girl and get back a dollar's worth.

"Huncle lived in three places; number 36 apartment with the clean lawn, sat up by the grand cemetery on the pothole road; on the street corner by the Second Drink, the bar with everybody outside yelling and swaying out the loud night time; and in the soft part up a woman legback, in the round wet pupils with dark holes, the hollow parts of her chest that beat quick at the look of snakes coming through the grass.

"Huncle was a diplomat, a quick pool player, a gardner and a Sunday school teacher; a Saturday's child, the sixth of seven

children, an uncle to 10 pickney, a lover to three women; a clean-hand man with no dirt under his nails, so he say."

Merle run a shaking finger down the thread, where it catch and rip, a ragged hole in the fabric. And Winsome go on reading it:

"*Come Christmas dinner a likkle pickney, dash herself behind window curtain, with belly full of pudding and cakes, sticky fruit fingers running down lace, eyes thick with up-past-bed-time. Behind the window curtain. And this is where she get caught. Huncle, clean-hand man, who like nothing better than a fully belly girl.*"

Merle stagger back, her leg splash in the water, and her body gone stiff. She fall on her heels and them catch her. Her eye roll back and she wail and cry. She wail out to the sky. Shaking her back from head to hip.

What she do to deserve such a son? Such a man as this. Her baby boy come to meet he judgement time.

Merle hand a shake and she reach out to he. Naked soul spread out across the rock. She hold the twisted thread in her hand, fresh and wet like the first day he born. Her mouth gone dry and she look to him.

"Wickedness. It come and it go. No saying when or why," she say slow.

And then she ring him quick like a snap neck.

Sarah Tolmie

PRECOR

Sabrina was sure she was one of the few members of her gym who knew that the name on all the treadmills and ellipticals – Precor – was Latin for *please*, or *I beseech you*. The person who named the company had known, of course. A small cabal of Latinists is kept hidden away in the corporate world for such things. Hence, for example, Telus, a fairly recherché poetic word for *world*. These names are not accidents. Sabrina thought of the ironic snicker somebody had uttered over *precor*. Precor is deponent: passive for active. Here we all are, running our asses off, passive forms pretending to be active. I beseech you, fitness gods! These were the thoughts that ran through her mind as she stalked grimly on and on, not going anywhere. She had been at this – the gym, the treadmill – for three weeks, following on from some unusually apocalyptic statements from her diabetes doctor. Her pace was steady: slow and resigned.

On this particular day, a Wednesday in mid-June, her feet began to behave erratically. She was annoyed. She could hardly go any slower. What was going on? She had half an hour to go. Please, please, please, just let me get this done. Precor!

At this, she felt a tremor or flutter in her head. She tried to stop walking, fearful that she was having a stroke. But her feet would not stop. They carried on walking. They felt lighter and smaller and closer to her centre of gravity, as if she had shrunk.

But there they were, her own feet, size eight, in cheap sneakers, the same distance away as usual. She experienced a sudden moment of vertigo and clutched the armrests, expecting to trip and stagger. But she did not stagger. Her strangely light feet walked on, toes turned out more than usual. They seemed to scuff the ground, though she was on the rubbery treadmill surface. She was tired. She was distraught. Maybe her blood sugar was crashing. She insisted to her feet that they stop walking. They did not stop. They walked a little faster; they began to skip.

Sabrina could not remember the last time she had skipped. Decades ago. Yet here she was, skipping plumply along on the treadmill on a Wednesday afternoon without the slightest intention of doing so. She had been possessed by a skipping demon. She tried to quell a rising panic. She determined to get off the treadmill. This was difficult to do as she could not stop skipping. Finally she succeeded, though her repeated attempts attracted the attention of the rapt, aloof women whizzing along beside her in their earbuds. She returned their stony glances, trying to make it appear that she, too, was receiving some sort of healthful instruction – in her case, about relentless skipping – through earbuds. She skipped off down the line of machines, holding on to the wall. People are used to bizarre movements in gyms and no one seemed to remark on her. Her light feet skipped on. Her heart thundered. Her forearms felt chilled. She felt an anxiety attack coming on. Stop, please, please just stop whatever this is! – her mind wailed – *please*!

Her feet stopped skipping. They walked. They walked rapidly, lightly, somehow expectantly. *Yes, please. Please. Give me some.* So she thought. Her feet stopped. She was in the change room. She was exhausted and trembling. What had she thought? Sounds were left, already fading, a language she did not know: *Bale, tkaya. Tkaya. Handakm bdare.* It wasn't Arabic. Turkish? Her brain seized on this philological musing like a lifeline. Businesslike, she transcribed what she remembered phonetically into her notes app, then sat, still trembling, on a bench. She looked suspiciously down at her feet. The silver logo on each shoe shone innocently. Her feet rested on the patterned floor next to one another and did nothing untoward. She was afraid to move. After a few deep breaths she tried moving one, then the other. All seemed well. She dismissed the idea of taking a shower, not without resentment – the gym showers had rich suburban water pressure that her shabby genteel plumbing could not match – because the idea of some further rebellion from her extremities while she was wet and naked on a slippery floor was too scary. Was she safe to drive? No, she definitely was not. She left the car and took a cab home. She told her husband she'd had a dizzy spell and he picked it up later.

Her feet behaved normally for two weeks. This was more than she could say for her blood sugar. Finally she was driven back to the gym. She chose a different treadmill and began her slow and steady walking, apprehensively, clutching the machine's armrests. She tried to keep her eyes from reading the word Precor. But it was everywhere. Precor. Precor. Precor. All around her. She tried to watch the home renovation show on the screen in front of her but there wasn't enough to it to hold her attention. Precor. She walked on, nervously. Eventually she let go the arm rests. She had only 15 minutes to go. Please, just let me finish and get off this thing. Ten minutes. Please.

Her feet got light. They got small. She grabbed the armrests again as they gave the impression of sliding vertiginously toward her. But this time there was no skipping. The feet were tired. They were sore. They scuffed and dragged along. Altogether they felt weak, the feet. Sabrina, though terrified, was instantly worried. What was wrong with the feet? Feet! What's wrong? Who are you? Where are you? Can I help you? Please, tell me.

The feet at the end of her legs stumbled. They thought, *Tkaya, mn la to aparemawa, aw!* She understood it this time. The feet spoke Kurdish. She had spent quite a lot of time looking up elementary Kurdish phrases in the past two weeks. She had succeeded in identifying the transcription on her phone. It was all crazy and probably a hallucination, but she had still learned that *aw* meant *water*. *Aw, eau, aqua*: Indo-European. Kurdish. *Please, I beg you, water*.

Please! Where are you? What is your name? How old are you? Feet! Please, what can I—

Please, water.

The feet stopped. Sabrina had three minutes to go on her timer. She slid weirdly along the moving tread until she found the right button. She looked down at her still feet. The still feet. Exhaustion spread upward from them like a fume. She feared she would fall over. The feet could not support her weight.

The treadmill timer dinged triumphally. She stood on her own two feet once more. The small Kurdish feet were gone. Sabrina sat down on the unmoving tread and cried.

She came back every day after work for a month, walking, walking. Her family was surprised at her devotion. Her doctor was delighted. Sabrina lost weight, but she hardly noticed. She waited and waited for the little feet. They did not return.

She could not stand the empty treadmill any more, with only herself on it. She switched to the elliptical. There, endlessly climbing, she eventually became acquainted with a pair of Tibetan feet. These feet were older, tougher, seemingly tireless, laconic. Sometimes they ran uphill in bursts until she was breathless. From these feet, she learned the Tibetan words for *paper* and *border*. She wished these feet well. She entertained hopes for them.

From time to time she would go back to the treadmill. Please, please, please. Precor.

Susan Swan

THE OIL MAN'S TALE

1.

Outside the train window, pump jacks suddenly appear in the farmers' fields. We are entering oil country, the land of my youth. Oil was first discovered in southwestern Ontario, although the Indians had always known about it, and they used the gummy tar to seal leaks in their canoes.

I am going home because Mother claims Father was an impostor who did not own the oil wells that have made our family rich.

She says the evidence is in the old letters she has found hidden in the wall behind the chimney. Father installed a fake panel there when he built Craiglochie, our family estate. It is known in my hometown of Petrolia for its vast orchard of espaliered pear trees and Father's six-hole golf course where he used to amuse himself in the days when he was strong. Father is dead now and so cannot comment on the letters, nor solve the dilemma they present to Mother and myself.

I am the Liberal MP for the federal government, a foot soldier in the army of William Lyon Mackenzie King. I am no longer home except on holidays so Mother feels naturally alone and unsure how to handle such an unpleasant turn of events.

I have on my lap much correspondence to go through – several letters from farmers or their lawyers asking the government to fund the drainage of their farmlands. (Swamps are prevalent in Lambton County.) Then, too, a query from the party whip, asking if I intend to run again in the next election. His question is odd, considering the election is still three years off. Perhaps it is a tactful hint that I step down?

The letters from the citizens of my constituency will have to wait. With a sigh, I tuck them away and stare out the train window, where hundreds of pump jacks are bobbing like giant birds pecking the earth. They stretch to the horizon, a mechanical marvel bob-bob-bobbing away.

Nobody remembers the 1860s oil boom in our part of the world, nor do they recall Father's role in it. Indeed, Father used to complain how unfair it was of his fellow Yankees to say they had started the oil industry in North America when the first oil well was dug in 1857 in Oil Springs, Ontario, a year before the well in Titus, Pennsylvania.

As you might infer, Father was an opinionated man, a raconteur who talked about the old days with a shine in his eyes.

The idea of my parent being an imposter sets my teeth on edge, and I will have questions for Tim, the field hand, who will be waiting for me at the station in the Packard that Mother bought for her 65th birthday.

2.

Mother is still beautiful, although she has put on a great deal of weight. There are jokes among my uncles that she has come to resemble the Wife of Bath. It is true that she has acquired a double chin, but her friendly heart-shaped face is still pleasing, and her hair, shiny as if brand new, marches back from her head in silver rows, majestic and authoritative.

In Petrolia, Mother is well-known for her honesty and kindly ways. So it distresses me to see her weeping in relief as she greets me, her back to the living room with its stained oak floors and tall silk screens brought all the way from Shanghai. Behind her the fire crackles in our family hearth, which is a copy of the tiled hearths that Father saw once in Amsterdam.

Mother's home is her temple, and I am the temple dog guarding its riches. Mother decorated our house with Father's money, and nobody knows better than she how much it pleases me.

She kisses me warmly and leads me into the den where she hands me a metal box filled with old letters. The box was found in the cupboard behind the chimney.

"Do you remember the man who brought us the letters?" She turns her good ear toward me so she can understand my reply.

"Of course you don't," she says when I shake my head. "You were just a child the day he came to see us."

"Do his letters say Father was an imposter?"

"His letters imply this, yes. And I'm taking steps to learn the truth." She hesitates. "But you should read his letters before we talk."

"Mother? I've come a long way, and I am famished."

"You poor darling, well, come along. I had Bessie prepare your favourite meal." Mother rings a silver dinner bell and Bessie appears, stooped and smiling.

It is only later, much later after I have drunk too much of Mother's claret and supped like a lord on duck à l'orange that I bring out the letters. There are five and they are not long.

I seat myself in the padded armchair by my bedroom window and open the metal box the letters were found in. There is something familiar about the box, although I cannot think what.

3.

Oil Springs, Canada West,
June 28, 1862.

Dear Jeffrey: I have become a hard oiler as they call men like me in Oil Springs. I have a new friend who has promised to help me. His name is Van Bartley and he says oil will make us so rich we will lounge about like Sultans, our heads cooled by palm fronds waved by beautiful serving girls.

Van was the cook on our lumber scow but he is an artist by trade. On the Erie Canal, he was always sketching the fancy, nickel-plated harnesses of the tow horses. He is blind in one eye, and has a delicate constitution. I have heard you say of a man like Van that he is "a green sort of fellow."

On Lake St. Clair, our lumber scow ran into an oil slick. Two gushers had blown in Oil Springs, and the filthy tar poured down the rivers and streams on the Canadian side faster than the men could store it.

In the marshlands the tall reed grasses lay flattened under the weight of the oil. All manner of water birds were coated in the filthy stuff and the crew and I used pike poles to dispatch the rattlesnakes that crawled onto the deck to escape it.

Van and me were eager to find the source of the oil that caused the slick on Lake St. Clair. So in Wilkesport, we jumped ship and headed for Black Crik Trail, which takes you to Oil Springs.

Toward the middle of the afternoon, we followed a path out of the Forrest and came upon a most fantastical sight. We were looking at the geysers that had blown the oil into the creeks running down to the lake. Men have been digging in Oil Springs since 1855, and before me stretched an open plain with the remarkable signs of their industriousness!

We saw a farmwife dip a garment into the oil at her feet and wring it out into a wooden bucket. By her side, a girl stood up to her hips in sludge, striving to fill the same bucket with oil that she was collecting in a man's boot. Every time the girl lifted up her boot, oil ran out a hole in the boot's sole, wasting as much as it gave. While I stared at this whimsical sight, Van grabbed a tin cup and ran down to join the girl, hollering that he would drink a cup of skunk juice if her mother would pay him a dollar.

Your loving brother,
Chas

4.

Father often talked about the great oil slick on Lake St. Clair and how it was like a trail of black gold leading him to his fortune in Oil Springs. He said the slick had been so thick it had stopped shipping on the Upper Lakes. Their lumber scow had to anchor on the Canadian side before it went upriver to Wilkesport, and he enjoyed telling me the story of how he and a friend hid in the bushes while the crew went to the tavern. All night they heard gunshots and hollering voices coming from the saloons. Oh, it was wild in those days, Father said. At dawn, their captain began calling their names. Finally, the man gave up and soon after, Father watched his lumber scow round a bend in the river and disappear.

I pick up the second letter with considerably more interest.

Oil Springs, Canada West,
July 13, 1862.

Dear Jeffrey: You have never seen a place like Oil Springs. It has 12 general stores, a cooperage, a newspaper office and 9 hotels. And every 5 minutes, a stagecoach goes back and forth from one end of town to another. There are also street lanterns lit by gas from the wells and a beautiful plank sidewalk made of white oak, but if you fall off, you will land in mud that leaves an oily stain on your clothes.

On Sunday, I take broken glass from the taverns to the glass factory near Brigden and exchange it for glass bottles, which I sell to the miners for 25 cents. I also help out on the rigs. A Yankee here named Fairbank has devised a method of pumping oil using a spider wheel and a system of jerker rods. This method pumps 25 oil wells at one time. No matter how many jerker rods you use, each one is connected to a single pump house and that is the beauty of it.

From Fairbank, I learnt that wasting crude after a well blows could be prevented with a 12-foot leather bag filled with flax seeds. The bag is wrapped around a two-and-a-half-inch pipe and the pipe is lowered down the hole. The moisture of the oil swells the bag of seeds to form a seal between the pipe and the side of the hole so the oil comes up through the pipe. Is this not an ingenious design?

I know you would marvel at all I am seeing because you taught me how to seal leaks in the hull of a canal boat so the pressure of incoming water draws handfuls of dried manure into the seams.

With fondest wishes,
Chas

5.

Ah. I have finished the first two letters and now I understand why Mother is worried. Father expressed himself with fanciful words, and these letters are filled with plain-spoken descriptions of Yankee know-how. What's more, the stories he told never dwelt on practical matters like the old-fashioned jerker rods that we still use to this day on our oilfields. They are connected to a single pump house, and when you walk in our oil fields the sight of the jerker rods is what draws your eye: hundreds upon hundreds of horizontal wooden sticks sliding noisily back and forth above the ground. I am bewildered by Father's enthusiastic descriptions in his letter because he was never interested in our jerker rod system, or for that matter, the way a swollen seed bag could keep the oil from being wasted. Father preferred to recite "The Song of Hiawatha" by Henry Wadsworth Longfellow, and he never deigned to ask Mother about the rigs.

Is it possible Father developed his dreamy inclinations once he struck oil? It has been known to happen. The human personality is inventive when its survival is challenged. But once the challenge has been met, it can blossom into artistic expression. So perhaps that was the case with Father, who was forever painting and drawing while Mother and Tim, the field hand, ran McGill Oil.

6.

I start on the third letter, and then put it down, smiling. How could I have forgotten? I met the man these letters are addressed to when I was nine. His name was Jeffrey McGill. The year was

1892, and I was helping Mother hang an oil painting Father had made of the main street in Petrolia. It was the last picture he painted before the bad business with the nitroglycerine.

Mother invited Jeffrey McGill for iced tea on the verandah, and he sat down, mopping his face with a handkerchief. Father was resting, Mother said. She explained that Father has not been in his right mind since he was injured.

"My husband is not very handy," she said. "And he had the misfortune to be shooting a well near here when the dynamite went off. It was the last of his accidents, the poor lamb."

"You say Chas is not handy?" Mr. McGill sounded surprised.

Mother smiled. "My husband is a dreamer. I am more practical and together we have made a good home for our son." Her gaze drifted off to the oil derricks beyond the family pond and then rested on me. I was sitting on the porch swing, holding my toy sailboat.

"This is Chas Junior," my mother said. "He takes after his father."

Jeffrey McGill looked searchingly at my face. "I cannot see the likeness," he remarked. "But I am most eager to see my brother, Mrs. McGill. It has been 30 years since I heard from him."

"Chas wrote you?" Mother looked puzzled. "He never told me he had an older brother."

"My brother's letters stopped in December, 1862. I couldn't leave home to come north and find out why. I own canal boats on Lake Champlain, and my business left me no time for such journeys."

"You say my husband's letters stopped in December 1862?" Mother asked. "In December his best friend, Van Bartley, drowned in an oil well."

Mr. McGill stared off at the pump jacks going up and down in the meadows. He seemed unhappy to hear Mother's news. "My brother has done well for himself," he said finally.

"Are you in need of money?" Mother asked.

He shook his head vigorously. "I was the one who financed my brother's trip to Oil Springs."

"So you think you deserve a share in what he found?" Mother replied, a quaver in her voice.

"Mrs. McGill, my doctor says I have only a few months to live so I have come to say goodbye to Chas."

Mother and I stared at him curiously. It was true he did not look well. His eyes were ringed with black circles and moisture dripped from his face as if the man was overcome by the tropical heat that used to be common in Petrolia 350 million years ago, when McGill oil was being made.

"Please ma'am," he said. "Can I see Chas?"

He looked at Mother so bespeechingly she took my hand and the three of us went into the second parlour where she had set up Father's bed. I was used to the pitiful sight Father made lying on his mattress. He slept downstairs because he no longer had the strength to climb up to his bedroom on the third floor.

"Is he blind in that eye?" Jeffrey McGill whispered, looking at Father's eyepatch.

"Yes, and now he can no longer speak," Mother replied. "But if you ask him a question, he will write his answer on the slate by his bed."

Jeffrey McGill came close to Father and said: "I am your brother, Jeffrey. Do you remember me? Thirty years have passed since you and I saw each other."

Father buried his head under his pillow, groaning so Mr. McGill suggested he read some of the letters he brought with him to help Father remember.

Mother nodded and, in a calm, reassuring voice, Jeffrey McGill started reading out loud. Immediately, Father began to wail piteously and Mother rushed to his side.

"You have frightened him," Mother cried.

"I am trying to learn the truth," Jeffrey McGill retorted. "My brother was not blind in one eye."

"You haven't seen him in 30 years." Mother spoke loudly so she could be heard above the noise of Father's cries. "Now I must ask you to leave."

"I tell you this man is not Chas." Jeffrey McGill gripped Mother by her shoulders. "I'll know it's Chas if you let me see his feet."

"Sir, you forget yourself," Mother replied, shaking free of his hands. "Please go this instant."

7.

I had forgotten Jeffrey McGill's peculiar request to see Father's feet. Not only did he want to see Father's feet, he asked to see mine. But I am getting ahead of myself.

Oil Springs, Canada West,
October 9, 1862.

Dear Jeffrey:

Van's scheme to sell cardboard patterns for men's shirts is a failure. The farmwomen here close their doors on strangers thinking they are hooligans from the taverns at Wilkesport. So Van is discouraged and often complains that our digestive powers have suffered from drinking out of the oily stream. He wants to go to Pennsylvania where he says the oil does not stink of sulphur the way it does here.

To make matters worse, Van was kicked out of our hotel for picking a fight with one of our bunkmates.

So we have put up a shanty on a ½ acre lot sold to me by a local shepherd. The smoke goes directly up and out a hole in the roof, and we sleep on hemlock boughs. We have nicknamed our quarters McGill's Folly and when I strike oil, I will make McGill's Folly a mansion fit for a president.

Every day, Van goes to the tavern while I help other men with their oil rigs, and every night I stuff my boots with oak leaves to soften their soles, which are worn through from the action of my foot on the treadle. Digging with a treadle takes a physical toll on a man like myself, with his monster toes. They swell up at night and cause me no end of pain. Blast the ancestor who gave us this deformity!

Your brother,
Chas

8.

Jeffrey McGill's peculiar question about seeing Father's feet came up again shortly after we left Father's bedroom.

"Did he never speak of having a brother then?" Mr. McGill asked Mother in the hallway.

She hesitated.

I could tell she was trying to remember.

I caught the stranger's eye and said: "Father told me he had a younger brother in Detroit."

Jeffrey McGill stood still as can be. "I am living proof that is not so," he replied.

"Chas, please go outside and play with your sailboat," Mother said fiercely.

I did as I was told and a few minutes later, Jeffrey McGill came down our verandah steps and over to where I stood in Father's fountain, sailing my boat. By then, I had taken off my boots and rolled up my pants, and he asked me to come out of the water so he could see something.

As we stood talking, I could hear the familiar creak-creak-creak of the jerker rods in the nearby oil fields. The sound always made me think of the tales by Edgar Allan Poe that Mother read me at bedtime, and that afternoon, while I chatted with our visitor, I felt myself shiver.

"What do you want to see?" I asked.

"Your toes," he replied. "I want to see if they are like mine."

I felt shy about showing him my feet so I stayed in the pool.

"The toes of the men in my family are webbed," he said. "I wondered if yours are the same."

With that, I lifted my foot out of the water and showed it to Jeffrey McGill.

"So you do not share our family trait." He looked so angry I felt afraid.

At that moment, Mother appeared. "Mr. McGill, why are you still here talking to my boy? I asked you to leave."

"The man you call your husband is not Chas. And here is my proof!" He waved the letters as if he was wielding a scythe to cut Mother down. "It means your oil wells belong to me."

"You are a fortune hunter," she cried.

"And you, madam, are living off property that isn't yours," he retorted.

"That's a lie," Mother replied. "I am an honest woman." She began to weep.

"Don't be mean to Mummy," I said, tugging at his jacket.

He looked ashamed of himself. "If you read the letters you will come to the same conclusion I have." He handed Mother the letters. "Your husband is an imposter who somehow got his hands on my brother's wells."

He swung himself up on his horse. "I will come back for the letters in two days and then you and I will have a talk, Mrs. McGill." He looked down at me, smiling. "And if you really are Chas's boy, you will grow up to be a good man."

9.

Here are the last letters to Jeffrey McGill, with their claim to our home and oil fields.

Oil Springs, Canada West,
October 29, 1862.

Dear Jeffrey: Yesterday Van and me had a fight. He has gone to Brigden to live with a farmwife, and I am back "canalling" again. The autumn rains have arrived, and I spend my days up to my waist dragging stone boats to the railroad station in Wyoming. You would be astonished to see me working in "the canal," as they call the slick muddy path that runs through the Great Swamp of Enniskillen. Each stone boat has a flat bottom and can hold two thirty-five-gallon barrels of oil. At night, I wash my clothes in the crik by our shanty and am too exhausted to talk.

Your brother,
Chas

Oil Springs, Canada West,
Dec. 16, 1862.

Dear Jeffrey: An oil smeller has divined oil at the bottom of my hillock. I have named the well Old Shepherd after the shepherd who sold me my lot and I spend up to 18 hours every day jigging down.

Alas, I have parted ways with Van for good. He is drinking more every day, and when I hit a gusher, he says he wants his share because he helped me establish myself in Oil Springs. I have told him that he will get nothing from me. He spends all his days in the tavern and has not put in one hour on my oil rigs.

Tomorrow I expect my rig to reach a depth of 130 feet. My crew is prepared for the well to blow, and I have warned them to stand back because dangerous gases come up with the oil. Men have died after being overwhelmed by the noxious fumes.

If anything happens to me, I am leaving the oil well to you, Jeffrey. I have commissioned a photographer to do my portrait and the law firm Bradford & Son has drawn up a will that states my intentions.

Your brother,
Chas

10.

Old letters are not corroborating evidence. Nevertheless, it's clear the man who wrote these letters wanted to leave his oil well to his brother, Jeffrey. It's far less clear who the man was. If he were the real Charles McGill, then who was Father? Van Bartley, the drunkard friend mentioned in the letters?

There are no more letters after this one. Is it possible their author fell into his well after being overcome by toxic fumes? Or is the truth something worse? What if Father pushed Charles McGill into the well? If Father is a murderer then we cannot retain any portion of Craiglochie with its prosperous oil fields.

But Father would never do something so cruel. It is more likely the oilman fell into the well by accident and Father thought he was doing nothing wrong when he claimed the land as his own. After all, Father was only 19 when he walked the Black Creek trail to Oil Springs. He was a young man wanting to get ahead the way young men have always done. So what was the harm in posing as the owner of his friend's well? How could he know the other man had bequeathed the oil well to his brother?

Yet, how terrible to think Father lied to us all these years! How terrible to consider the possibility that he was deliberately fooling Mother and me! Especially Mother, who waited on him hand and foot.

There is no point speculating. If what the letters say is true, we have two choices: we can give back the oil wells or pretend the letters don't exist and go on as before. After all, we are the ones who planted the pear orchards and built the oil derricks. We are also the ones who pay the men on the rigs. And we are the ones who give daily business to the shop owners in these parts. Why should we have to hand over the fruits of our labours?

Yes, why should we hand over our property to someone who won't run the oil rigs as successfully as Mother and Tim? Who would neglect our well-tended pear orchards? I can't move Mother out of her home at her age! My small apartment in Ottawa isn't up to her standards. She has been raised to be a hostess of a grand establishment like Craiglochie. She won't know what to make of Ottawa, where the politicians eat each other for breakfast.

I will talk to William Lyon about this mess. He won't let me down. I'm one of his upcoming younger members. Just a few weeks ago, he hinted about giving me a cabinet post. In the meantime, I have remembered the rest of Jeffrey McGill's visit and how the letters came to be in the chimney.

11.

After Jeffrey McGill departed from Petrolia, Mother sat on the front porch clutching the letters. She looked as sad as she did the day Father was harmed in the nitroglycerine explosion.

"Are you going to read them?" I asked.

"Not yet." Mother sighed. "Chas, I will go for a walk first and clear my head."

When I asked if I could come with her, she told me she needed to be alone so she could collect herself. She often walked in the oil fields when she felt discouraged. She said the creaking noise of the jerker rods proves there will always be money for us, even if God decides to take Father up to Heaven.

When I could see her walking among the jerker rods, I snatched up the letters, praying she would not return and catch me. I put the letters in a metal box I stole from Father's studio and hid the box in the secret panel in the chimney. It was the panel that Father used to stash his liquor. I caught him doing it once and he swore me to secrecy.

I was in bed by the time Mother came back from her walk. She peered in the door of my bedroom and asked if I knew what had happened to the letters.

"Did you take them?" she said.

"Mother, I cannot read very well," I reminded her.

"Ah, that's right," she replied. "What would you want with a bunch of old letters?"

The next day she asked Bessie and Tim, the farmhand, but neither of them had seen Jeffrey McGill's letters. Later that day Jeffrey McGill sent word that he had to return home on unexpected business, and he asked Mother to return his letters in the post.

Father died soon after, and Mother was too busy with the funeral to think any more about the letters. Then one of Jeffrey McGill's relatives sent us word that he had died of heart failure.

12.

So now here I am, back in my childhood bedroom at Craiglochie, wondering what to tell Mother. As if on cue, she opens the door, an oil lamp in her hand. When I nod in friendly fashion, she limps toward me in her buttoned boots and peers up at my face.

"The town clerk is downstairs. He has found an old will at city hall by a man named Charles McGill."

"You told the clerk about the letters?" I cry. "Without asking me?

"It was the right thing to do," she says stubbornly. As I try to argue her out of her idiotic idea, a shower of light fills the room. In astonishment, we turn towards the window.

Outside, the moon is rising over the pear orchards. It has come up suddenly, the way it does in the countryside. Oh, how I have loved Craiglochie – the meadows where bluebirds nest on our fence posts; the large, screened-in verandah where Mother and I take afternoon tea; the Staffordshire firedogs, the dark red porcelain lamps from China, the stately butler's chair with its wooden wings, the spool beds custom designed for us in New York.

Mother puts a finger to her lips and whispers: "*Ssssh,* Chas. Do you hear something?" Mother is somewhat deaf, and she is often confused by unexpected noises. We both listen. At first, I hear nothing because the sound is so familiar. Then, as if to mock me, comes the creak of the wooden jerker rods hauling our oily treasure out of the earth.

Katie Zdybel resides in the Blue Mountains region of Ontario. "The Critics" and "Honey Maiden" (from this collection) appear in two issues of *EXILE Quarterly*, and other stories have been published in *The Antigonish Review, Prairie Journal,* and *The Malahat Review.* She has an MFA in Creative Writing from UBC, and is also a graduate of the Humber College Creative Writing by Correspondence program. *Equipoise* is her first collection of stories, was produced with the assistance of a Canada Council for the Arts grant, and was published by Exile Editions in 2021.

photo by Sarah Tacoma

Linda Rogers of Victoria, British Columbia, began writing short stories at the behest of Exile's publisher, who told her it would be fun. He was right. Rogers writes fiction, non-fiction, poetry, and songs with her husband, blues mandolinist Rick van Krugel. She is the recipient of, among others, the Leacock, Kenney, Montreal Poetry, Livesay, Bridport, Cardiff, and MacEwen Awards for writing. Linda has been a Canadian People's Poet, a Victoria Poet Laureate, the president of the League of Canadian Poets and the Federation of BC Writers, and an honorary Arts Citizen of Victoria. Her most recent books are the short story collection, *Crow Jazz*, and the novels, *Bozuk* and *Repairing the Hive*. She is currently editing a collection of women's art and writing, *Mother, the Verb*.

photo by Veronique da Silva

Susan Swan is a critically acclaimed writer who has been published in 18 countries and translated into eight languages. In 2019, she published her eighth book of fiction, *The Dead Celebrities Club*. Swan's 2012 novel, *The Western Light*, was a prequel to *The Wives of Bath*, her international bestseller made into the feature film *Lost and Delirious*, which premiered at Sundance and was shown in 32 countries. Her 2004 novel, *What Casanova Told Me,* was a finalist for the Commonwealth Writers' Prize. Her award winning first novel, *The Biggest Modern Woman of the World*, about a Canadian giantess who exhibited with P.T. Barnum, is currently being made into a television series. Swan is a retired Humanities professor from York University, and lives in Toronto.

A.S. Penne of Sechelt, British Columbia, is the author of two books and numerous fiction and nonfiction works published in literary journals, periodicals, and anthologies. Most recently a writer for the stage, she used a chapter from her literary nonfiction title, *Old Stones*, to create the stage play, *Coming Back*. She has won the UK's Ian St James Award and the U.S. Writers' Digest award. In Canada her work has been a finalist in CBC's Canada Writes, the Western Magazine Awards, and the Norma Epstein Creative Writing Competition.

photo by Anna Wright

Christine Ottoni of Toronto has had short fiction appear in *The Nashwaak Review*, *The Alaska Quarterly Review*, *Riddle Fence*, *EXILE Quarterly*, and *PRISM international*. Her debut short story collection, *Cracker Jacks for Misfits*, was published with Exile Editions in 2019, and was shortlisted for the 2020 ReLit Award. www.christineottoni.com

photo by Christopher De Rosa

Kate Felix-Segriff is a writer and filmmaker based in Toronto. Her work has appeared in *Into the Void*, *Room Magazine*, *Cream City Review*, and others. Her feminist short films have been selected for over 50 film festivals world-wide and she recently won the Bumblebee Prize for Flash Fiction.

www.katefelix.com @kitty_flash on Twitter.

Darlene Madott is a Toronto lawyer and award-winning author of seven books, including *Making Olives and Other Family Secrets* which won the Bressani Literary Award in 2008, and *Stations of the Heart* (Exile Editions) again won the Bressani Award in 2014. This is her fourth time to be shortlisted for the CVC Award. In autumn 2021, Exile will publish *Dying Times*, a fictional exploration of the last journey. www.DyingTimes.com *photo by Vincenzo Pietropaolo*

Marion Quednau, of British Columbia's Sunshine Coast, has won acclaim for both her poetry and prose: the Malahat Long Poem Prize, a National Magazine Award, and the Smithbooks-Books in Canada First Novel award. Her work has appeared in various magazines and anthologies, and in the poetry collection, *Paradise, Later Years*. Her story, "Sunday Drive to Gun Club Road," is the title story for a short fiction collection released in 2021. *photo by Kat Wahamaa*

Lue Palmer is a writer of literary fiction, non-fiction and poetry, and an editorial board member at *Room Magazine* and *PREE Caribbean Literature*. Lue is a recipient of the Octavia E. Butler Memorial Scholarship, and an alumni of Clarion West 2021. Lue has also had the joy of attending the Bread Loaf Writers Conference and Banff Centre Writers Studio Residency. Published in North America and the Caribbean, Lue Palmer is completing their first novel, *The Hungry River*, and is grateful for the support of the Canada Council for the Arts and the Ontario Arts Council.

luepalmerwriter.com *photo by @RoyadelSol*

Sarah Tolmie is a speculative fiction writer, poet, and professor of English at the University of Waterloo. Her novel, *The Little Animals*, earned the Special Citation at the 2020 Philip K. Dick Awards, and her poetry collection, *The Art of Dying*, was a finalist for the 2019 Griffin Poetry Prize. Her experimental short fiction collection, *Disease* (which includes the story "Precor"), was released late summer of 2020. In the fall of 2020 her novella, *The Fourth Island*, and her third poetry collection, *Check*, were released. (Credit: The Kurdish in "Precor" was provided by Media Hawezi.) www.sarahtolmie.ca

photo by Scott Straker

Equipoise was shortlisted for the HarperCollins/UBC Prize for Best New Fiction, and is Katie Zdybel's first book.

"I admire Katie Zdybel's incisive, pared-down prose, her insights into womanhood, family, and friendships." —Joyce Carol Oates

"This is the best collection of domestic short fiction, each phrase so aptly tuned to each emotion, that I have read since Alice Munro's *Too Much Happiness*." —Janet Somerville, author of *Yours, for Probably Always, Martha Gellhorn's Letters of Love and War, 1930–1949*

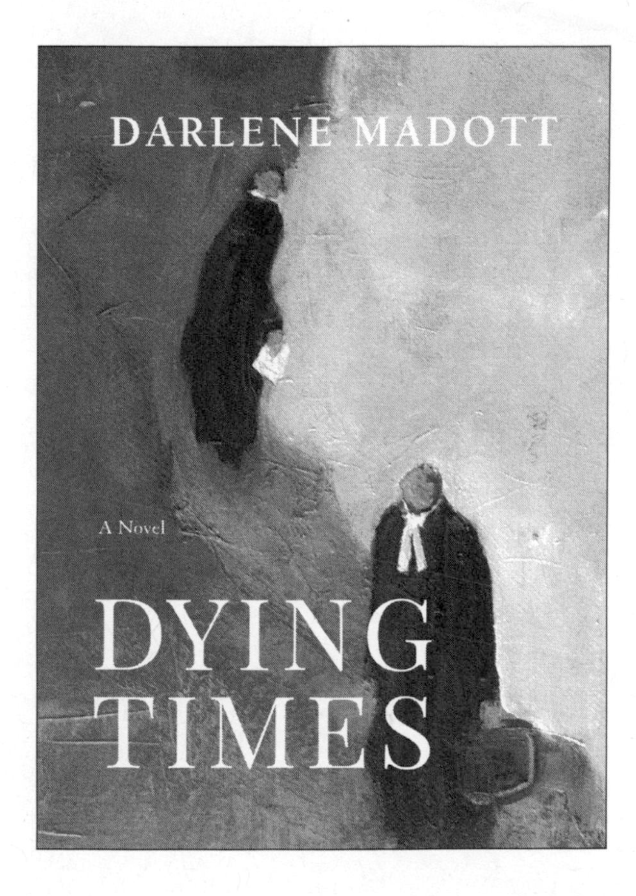

"Darlene Madott is snared in a spiderweb of rivalry, resentment and grief in this wise and compelling meditation on death, loss and forgiveness. The deaths of her aged parents, the demise of her mentor and legal partner, and her decision to retire after decades as a successful lawyer in a male-dominated legal firm, precipitate a moral and emotional crisis. She wants to move forward but first she must escape the entangling tendrils of rage and bitterness that trap her in ancient feuds with a diabolical sibling, a deadbeat former husband, an avaricious client and jealous colleagues. How to forgive and forgo so she can find harmony in the last part of her life is the dilemma animating this treatise on love and forgiveness. Written in a frank and crisp style, *Dying Times* offers compelling life lessons for the young as well as the aged. I couldn't put it down." —Sandra Martin of the *Globe and Mail*, and author of *A Good Death* and *Working the Dead Beat.*

CVC8:

Leanne Milech – "The Light in the Closet"
(winner, Emerging Writer – Toronto, Ontario)
Edward Brown – "Remember Me"
(co-winner, Any Career Point Writer – Toronto, Ontario)
Priscila Uppal – "Elevator Shoes"
(co-winner, Any Career Point Writer – Toronto, Ontario)

• Shortlisted:
Cara Marks– "Aurora Borealis"
(Victoria, British Columbia)
William John Wither – "The Bulbous It with No Eyelids"
(London, Ontario)
Mark Paterson – "My Uncle, My Barbecue Chicken Deliveryman"
(Lorraine, Quebec)
Lorna Crozier – "Rebooting Eden"
(Vancouver Island, British Columbia)
Bruce Meyer – "Cantique de Jean Racine"
(Barrie, Ontario)
Christine Miscione – "Your Failing Heart."
(Hamilton, Ontario)
Martha Bátiz – "Suspended"
(Richmond Hill, Ontario)
Andrea Bradley – "No One Is Watching"
(Oakville, Ontario)

CVC7:

Halli Villegas – "Road Kill"
(winner, Emerging Writer – Mount Forest, Ontario)
Seán Virgo – "Sweetie"
(winner, Any Career Point Writer – Eastend, Saskatchewan)

• Shortlisted:
Iryn Tushabe – "A Separation"
(Saskatchewan)
Katherine Fawcett – "The Pull of Old Rat Creek"
(Squamish, British Columbia)
Darlene Madott – "Winners and Losers"
(Toronto, Ontario)
Jane Callen – "Grace"
(Victoria, British Columbia)
Yakos Spiliotopoulos – "Grave Digger"
(Toronto, Ontario)
Chris Urquhart – "Skinbound"
(Toronto, Ontario)
Norman Snider – "Husband Material"
(Toronto, Ontario)
Carly Vandergriendt – "Resurfacing"
(Montreal, Quebec)
Linda Rogers – "Breaking the Sound Barrier"
(Victoria, British Columbia)

CVC6:

Matthew Heiti – “For They Were Only Windmills”
(winner, Emerging; Sudbury, Ontario)
Helen Marshall – “The Gold Leaf Executions”
(winner, Any Career Point; Sarnia, Ontario/Cambridge, U.K.)

• Shortlisted:
Diana Svennes-Smith – “Stranger In Me”
(Eastend, Saskatchewan)
Sang Kim – “Kimchi”
(Toronto, Ontario)
A.L. Bishop – “Hospitality”
(Niagara Falls, Ontario)
Katherine Govier – “Elegy: Vixen, Swan, Emu”
(Toronto, Ontario)
Sheila McClarty – “The Diamond Special”
(Oakbank, Manitoba)
Caitlin Galway – “Bonavere Howl”
(Toronto, Ontario)
Bruce Meyer – “The Slithy Toves”
(Barrie, Ontario)
Frank Westcott – “It Was a Dark Day - Not a Stormy Night - In Tuck-Tea-Tee-Uck-Tuck”
(Alliston, Ontario)
Martha Bátiz – “Paternity, Revisited”
(from Mexico; lives Richmond Hill, Ontario)
Leon Rooke – “Open the Door”
(Toronto, Ontario)
Norman Snider – “How Do You Like Me Now?”
(Toronto, Ontario)

CVC5:

Lisa Foad – "How To Feel Good"
(winner, Emerging; Toronto, Ontario)
Nicholas Ruddock – "Mario Vargas Llosa"
(winner, Any Career Point; Guelph, Ontario)

• Shortlisted:
Hugh Graham – "After Me"
(Toronto, Ontario)
Josip Novakovich – "Dunavski Pirat"
(from Croatia; lives Montreal, Quebec)
Leon Rooke – "Sara Mago et al"
(Toronto, Ontario)
Jane Eaton Hamilton – "The Night SS Sloan Undid His Shirt"
(Vancouver, British Columbia)
Bruce Meyer – "Tilting"
(Barrie, Ontario)
Priscila Uppal – "Bed Rail Entrapment Risk Notification Guide"
(Toronto, Ontario)
Christine Miscione – "Spring"
(Hamilton, Ontario)
Veronica Gaylie – "Tom, Dick, and Harry"
(Vancouver, British Columbia)
Maggie Dwyer – "Chihuahua"
(Commanda, Ontario)
Bart Campbell – "Slim and The Hangman"
(Vancouver, British Columbia)
Linda Rogers – "Raging Breath and Furious Mothers"
(Victoria, British Columbia)
Lisa Pike – "Stellas"
(Windsor, Ontario)

CVC4:

Jason Timermanis – "Appetite"
(winner, Emerging; Toronto, Ontario)
Hugh Graham – "The Man"
(winner, Any Career Point; Toronto, Ontario)

• Shortlisted:
Helen Marshall – "The Zhanell Adler Brass Spyglass"
(Sarnia, Ontario)
K'ari Fisher – "Saddle Up!"
(Burns Lake, British Columbia)
Linda Rogers – "Three Strikes"
(Victoria, British Columbia)
Susan P. Redmayne – "Baptized"
(Oakville, Ontario)
Matthew R. Loney – "The Pigeons of Peshawar"
(Toronto, Ontario)
Erin Soros – "Morning is Vertical"
(Vancouver, British Columbia)
Gregory Betts – "Planck"
(St. Catharines, Ontario)
George McWhirter – "Sisters in Spades"
(Vancouver, British Columbia)
Madeline Sonik – "Punctures"
(Victoria, British Columbia)
Leon Rooke – "Slain By a Madam"
(Toronto, Ontario)

CVC3:

Sang Kim – "When John Lennon Died"
(winner, Emerging; Toronto, Ontario)
Priscila Uppal – "Cover Before Striking"
(co-winner, Any Career Point; Toronto, Ontario)
Austin Clarke – "They Never Told Me"
(co-winner, Any Career Point; Toronto, Ontario)

• Shortlisted:
George McWhirter – "Tennis"
(Vancouver, British Columbia)
David Somers – "Punchy Sells Out"
(Winnipeg, Manitoba)
Leon Rooke – "Conditional Sphere of Everyday Historical Life"
(Toronto, Ontario)
Helen Marshall – "Lessons in the Raising of Household Objects"
(Sarnia, Ontario)
Yakos Spiliotopoulos – "Black Sheep"
(Toronto, Ontario)
Greg Hollingshead – "Mother / Son"
(Toronto, Ontario)
Matthew R. Loney – "A Fire in the Clearing"
(Toronto, Ontario)
Rob Peters – "Sam's House"
(Vancouver, British Columbia)
Liz Windhorst Harmer – "Teaching Strategies"
(Hamilton, Ontario)

CVC2:

Christine Miscione – “Skin, Just”
(winner, Emerging; Hamilton, Ontario)
Leon Rooke – “Here Comes Henrietta Armani”
(co-winner, Any Career Point; Toronto, Ontario)
Seán Virgo – “Gramarye”
(co-winner, Any Career Point; East End, Saskatchewan)

• Shortlisted:
Kelly Watt – “The Things My Dead Mother Says”
(Flamborough, Ontario)
Darlene Madott – “Waiting (An Almost Love Story)”
(Toronto, Ontario)
Linda Rogers – “Darling Boy”
(Victoria, British Columbia)
Daniel Perry – “Mercy”
(Toronto, Ontario)
Amy Stuart – “The Roundness”
(Toronto, Ontario)
Phil Della – “I Did It for You”
(Vancouver, British Columbia)
Jacqueline Windh – “The Night the Floor Jumped”
(Vancouver, British Columbia)
Kris Bertin – “Tom Stone and Co.”
(Halifax, Nova Scotia)
Martha Bátiz – “The Last Confession”
(Richmond Hill, Ontario)

CVC1:

Silvia Moreno-Garcia – “Scales as Pale as Moonlight”
(co-winner, Emerging; Vancouver, British Columbia)
Frank Westcott – “The Poet”
(co-winner, Emerging; Shelburne Ontario)
Ken Stange – “The Heart of a Rat”
(winner, Any Career Point; Toronto, Ontario)

• Shortlisted:
Hugh Graham – “Through the Sky”
(Toronto, Ontario)
Leigh Nash – “The Field Trip”
(Toronto, Ontario)
Rishma Dunlop – “Paris”
(Toronto, Ontario)
Zoe Stikeman – “Single-Celled Amoeba”
(Toronto, Ontario)
Kristi-ly Green – “The Patient”
(Toronto, Ontario)
Gregory Betts – “To Tell You”
(Oakville Ontario)
Richard Van Camp – “On the Wings of This Prayer”
(Edmonton, Alberta)

Christine Ottoni has crafted a finely layered narrative of interconnected short stories about discovering independence, strength, and the power to love in which Naomi, Joanne, Jake, and Marce find themselves caught in the crosshairs of modern-day chaos marked by urban claustrophobia and loneliness. *Cracker Jacks for Misfits* is a contemporary and poignant portrait of the moment when childhood becomes a new country of adult commitments…